GRUMPY BOSS TROUBLE

By
Alex McAnders

McAnders Books

*****

The characters and events in this book are fictitious. Any similarity to real persons, living or dead, is coincidental and not intended by the author. The person or people depicted on the cover are models and are in no way associated with the creation, content, or subject matter of this book.

All rights reserved. No part of this book may be reproduced in any form or by any electronic or mechanical means, including information storage and retrieval systems, without permission in writing from the publisher, except by a reviewer who may quote brief passages in a review. For information contact the publisher at: McAndersPublishing@gmail.com.

Copyright © 2022

Official Website: www.AlexAndersBooks.com
Podcast: www.SoundsEroticPodcast.com
Visit Alex Anders
at: Facebook.com/AlexAndersBooks & Instagram
Get 6 FREE ebooks and an audiobook by signing up for Alex Anders' mailing list at: AlexAndersBooks.com

Published by McAnders Publishing

Titles by Alex McAnders

M/M Romance

Serious Trouble & Audiobook; Book 2 & Audiobook; Book 3 & Audiobook; Book 4 & Audiobook; Book 5
Serious Trouble - Graduation Day; Book 2; Book 3; Book 4
Mafia Billionaire Romance (MM)

*****

MMF Bisexual Romance

Searing Heet: The Copier Room; Hurricane Laine; Book 2; Book 3; Book 4; Book 5; Book 6

*****

Titles by A. Anders

MMF Bisexual Erotica

While My Family Sleeps; Book 2; Book 3; Book 4;
Book 1-4
Book 2
My Boyfriend's Twin; Book 2
My Boyfriend's Dominating Dad; Book 2

*****

MMF Bisexual Romance

Until Your Toes Curl: Prequels; Book 2; Book 3; Until Your Toes Curl
The Muse: Prequel; The Muse
Rules For Spanking
Island Candy: Prequel & Audiobook; Island Candy & Audiobook; Book 2; Book 2

In The Moonlight: Prequel; In The Moonlight & Audiobook
Aladdin's First Time; Her Two Wishes & Audiobook; Book 2 & Audiobook
Her Two Beasts
Her Red Hood
Her Best Bad Decision
Bittersweet: Prequel; Bittersweet
Before He Was Famous: Prequel; Before He Was Famous
Beauty and Two Beasts
Bane: Prequel & Audiobook; Bane & Audiobook
Bad Boys Finish Last
Aladdin's Jasmine
20 Sizzling MMF Bisexual Romances

*****

M/M Erotic Romance

Their First Time
Aladdin's First Time; Her Two Wishes & Audiobook; Book 2 & Audiobook

*****

Suspense

The Last Choice; Dying for the Rose
It Runs

*****

Titles by Alex Anders

MMF Bisexual Erotica

While My Family Sleeps; Book 2; Book 3; Book 4; Book 1-4
Dangerous Daddy's Double Team & Audiobook; Book 2

& Audiobook; Book 3 & Audiobook; Book 4 & Audiobook; Book 1-4
Black Magic Double Team & Audiobook

M/M Erotic Romance

Baby Boys
Baby Boy 1: Sacrificed; Book 2; Book 3; Book 4; Book 1-4

MMF Bisexual Romance

As My Rock Star Desires; Book 2; Book 3; Book 4; Book 5

GRUMPY BOSS TROUBLE

Chapter 1

Hil

"I think I just got someone killed," I said with the blood draining from my face.

"Hil, is that you?" Dillon's concern for my well-being was something I had grown to love him for.

"It's me. What have I done?"

"Where have you been? I've been worried sick! Where are you?"

"I'm in a hospital," I said, looking around at the other concerned people in the waiting room.

"No, I mean, what city are you in? Are you okay?"

"I'm fine. I lent someone my car, and they were in an accident. My phone got an alert saying it had been rear-ended and an ambulance had been called. Dillon, I think someone tried to run me off the side of a cliff."

"Hil, you have to tell me where you are."

"I don't know where I am. It's a small town in Tennessee. But I'm fine. I just needed to hear your voice. You can't tell anyone you've heard from me."

"Remy has been asking me about you. He said that your father is worried."

"You definitely can't tell him. Promise me you won't."

"Hil…"

"Promise me!"

"Okay. I promise. But you can't just disappear like that again."

"I won't. But I have to do this. I need to prove to them that I can make it on my own."

"Didn't you just say someone tried to run you off the side of a cliff?"

"I'll be fine, Dillon. I can do this."

"I was told that my mother was brought in," someone with the hottest southern accent said, pulling me away from my conversation with Dillon.

I looked up to see a guy at the reception desk twenty feet in front of me. He had jet-black hair, broad shoulders, and an athletic build. I could only see him from behind, but I was drawn to him. And when the guy who drove me to the hospital rushed to him, I got up to join them.

"I have to go."

"Don't disappear on me again. You have to tell me where you are."

"I'll call you soon. I promise, Dillon."

I ended the call and joined the two guys at the reception desk. Marcus, the one who had driven, turned to me as I did. "Hil, this is Cali. Dr. Sonya is his mother."

The taller built guy looked at me. As he did, my knees wobbled. There was something about his smell and the way his eyes peered into mine that made me weak.

"Why was my mother driving your car?" the gorgeous man snapped.

I stepped back, taken off guard. Certainly, I could understand why he would be upset. I might be too if I was in his situation. But couldn't he see that I was concerned as well?

"She had admired my car when I first arrived at the bed-and-breakfast. She had mentioned it a few times, so since I was supposed to be leaving today, I asked her if she'd like to take it for a drive. Should I not have? Is she not a good driver?"

Staring at me, Cali relented.

"No, that's fine. She's as good of a driver as anyone. You couldn't have known what would happen. I'm sorry, what was your name again?"

"It's Hilaire, but everyone calls me Hil," I said, offering him my hand.

Taking my small hand in his, he held it for longer than I had expected. The way he peered at me made me feel vulnerable. It was like he could see into me. I had no secrets when he looked at me like that.

"It's good to meet you, Hil. I guess I should apologize for what happened to your car."

"Don't be absurd. That's what insurance is for. I'm just hoping your mother will be alright."

Cali let go of my hand and turned away, breaking whatever connection we had. It hurt to feel it go. The downside to growing up the way I did is that I didn't get the chance to meet guys like Cali. As protective as my father was, I didn't go to school. I never had anything but tutors. I never got a life.

When my father figured out that I liked boys, he didn't make a big deal about it. But guys became another thing for him to protect me from. I felt like his little Princess. But not in the way that felt like I would find a Prince. It was in the way that told me that I couldn't be trusted to do anything. That was a part of the reason I was on this trip, to prove that I could survive on my own.

If I were being honest, another reason was that guys who looked like Cali, and made me feel the way he did, were far and few in between. At twenty years old, I was still a virgin. That would never change living under my father's protection. I had to get away. But now I was in a hospital in the middle of who-knows-where Tennessee, unsure of what to do, where to go, or how to get there.

"Thank you for coming, Marcus. But you don't have to stay. I'm sure you have a lot to do. I don't want to keep you from it," Cali said, not looking at him.

"No, I can be here for as long as you need me. She's your mother, but I cared about her too."

"Thank you. But Claudee and Titus will be here soon. There's no need for you to stay," the built guy said dismissively.

"No, seriously, I can stay as long as you need me."

Cali turned to face him with a look that could have been chiseled in marble.

"Marcus, go. I'll let you know how she's doing. I'm sure Hil will need a ride back as well."

I jolted back hearing my name said in the same dismissive tone. Did he not want us here? Was he upset with me because if it hadn't been for me, his mother wouldn't be in the state that she was?

I put my hand on Marcus's shoulder.

"We should go. I'm sure that Cali will update us when he knows more."

Cali turned to me with relief on his face. I wasn't sure why. Was there something going on between the two. Did they have history?

I turned back to Marcus to get a better look at him. He wasn't my type the way Cali was, but he was still very attractive. He was nowhere near as built as the

Adonis standing next to him, but he was fit and shared Cali's dimples.

"I can take you back to Dr. Sonya's," Marcus said, too sad to meet my eyes.

"Thank you," I said as if I didn't want to stay as much as he did.

"I'm sorry again about what happened to your mother," I said, capturing Cali's attention but not his gaze.

He barely acknowledged me. Staring at him, I desperately wanted to wrap my arms around him and tell him that his mother would be alright. But there was a prickly armor covering him that I couldn't penetrate.

Maybe he could see that I was gay and didn't like it. In the world I grew up in, hiding your weakness was the first step to survival. My attraction to guys was my weakness. At least, my father thought so. That was why I did my best to hide it.

Unfortunately, when I met guys who were hotter than sin, me hiding how I felt was like an elephant hiding behind a lamp pole. Cali is that hot. And maybe he doesn't like elephants.

Leaving as Cali requested, Marcus and I were silent as we drove back to the bed-and-breakfast. The entire way, he looked as confused by our interaction with Cali as I was. Cali didn't seem like a bad guy. Could he just not be very talkative? Did he have a history of being quiet?

Speaking of histories, did he and Marcus have one? Was there reason things seemed tense between the two? Had the two been sexual?

"I need to apologize for the way Cali reacted. He isn't usually so…" Marcus paused.

"Quick to get rid of people?"

Marcus laughed. "No, that part is typical Cali. He's usually a little nicer about it, though. You shouldn't take it personally."

"Do you?"

"Do I what?"

"Do you take it personally?"

Marcus's mouth opened, but he didn't speak. It took a while for him to say,

"Sometimes. He and I went to the same high school. Cali was on the football team and had girls throwing themselves at him. We didn't exactly hang out in the same circles.

"Our mothers are friends, so we were often forced to spend time together. I always felt like such an inconvenience for him. I guess nothing changes."

"So, Cali had a lot of girlfriends?" I asked, unable to hide my intent.

Marcus looked at me joining the long line of people who could see straight through me. He chuckled.

"Funny enough, although there was an endless line of girls after him, I never really saw him with any of them. He is more of a brooding, loner type."

"He mentioned two guys joining him. I take it that neither is a boyfriend?" I asked hesitantly.

Marcus laughed again.

"No, Claudee and Titus are his long-lost brothers."

"Long-lost brothers?"

"Yeah. Last fall, Titus's boyfriend passed around a DNA test and it turned out that the three of them share the same father."

"Oh, wow!"

"That's exactly what the rest of the town thought. It was a real scandal. Cali's mother was one of the people everyone couldn't stop talking about. 'Did the three of them all have the same father? How are they so close in age? Who was this man?'

"None of the mothers said. Supposedly, they wouldn't even tell their sons. Cali and Dr. Sonya we're pretty close until then. Now, Cali spends most of his time back at university."

"Cali attends college?"

"Yeah. He's on the football team. He and Titus both. Last season, Titus set the record for yards run in his position, and Cali set the record for yards kicked."

"That's an athletic family."

"Apparently," Marcus said with a painful ache in his eyes.

"I take it that you don't attend university?" I asked, assuming that he was around my age.

"I wasn't blessed with the natural ability that so many people in this town have. If it was in the water, I certainly didn't drink it," he said offering a smile.

"No, but I've tasted your pastries. You don't need to play football when you can make stuff that tastes like that. I know people who would kill for one of your chocolate croissants," I said genuinely.

Marcus blushed. It was enough to make me think that he was interested in me. It only took a moment of picturing him naked before realizing that I saw him more as a brother then someone I would want to get into bed with. Cali, though, just thinking about him felt like someone was squeezing my heart. Was this what it meant to ache for someone?

"I appreciate you saying that," Marcus said, pulling me from my increasingly elaborate fantasy of Cali. "Baking pastries is how I relax."

"I would trade an arm to be good at anything as much as you are at baking. I couldn't tell you how to boil an egg."

Marcus laughed. He must have thought I was joking. I wasn't. Growing up, we always had housekeepers and chefs. For a short while, we even had a food taster. It's a little hard to learn how to survive on your own when there is an endless supply of people who are paid to do things for you.

Switching topics for the remainder of our forty-five-minute drive, he told me about growing up in a small town. It was very different from how I grew up in New York. I asked him if he had ever caught fireflies in a mason jar. He laughed and said that he had.

"The next thing you're gonna tell me is that you and your friends would fish down at the creek."

He looked at me embarrassed.

"No, seriously?"

"You don't understand how few things there are to do here. But, have you ever tried it? It's actually pretty fun."

"I guess. It's got to be better than awkwardly pretending that you don't have a crush on any half-decent boy that your parents set you up on a play date with."

Marcus looked at me with realization.

"So, you're into guys?"

"If by into, you mean desperately longing to have one in me, then yes," I admitted with a smile.

"That's cool," he said, seeming to mean it.

"Clearly you've never been into guys," I laughed.

Marcus looked away without responding. There was something he wasn't saying. Maybe if I had had any opportunity to refine my gaydar, I would know what it was. The only other guy I knew who was into guys was Dillon, and he had as hard of a time hiding it as I did.

When we arrived back at the bed-and-breakfast, Marcus asked me if I would need anything now that I didn't have a car. I told him I would be fine. He then gave me his number and told me to call if I needed anything. I was grateful.

I was trying to be independent and self-reliant, but the truth was that I didn't know what I was doing. What was I going to do now that I didn't have a car? More than that, what was I going to do without cash?

If you're trying to take the kind of trip that I was, you can't rely on your father's credit card. Credit card purchases can be tracked. If I used it, my father would know exactly where I was.

Alternatively, you could take the family car that doesn't have a tracking device in it, pocket a few stacks of cash that your father keeps hidden around the house, shut off your phone, and go whatever you want.

That was the option I chose. But I also kept the cash in my car thinking that's where it would be safest. Should I have thought about that before allowing Dr. Sonya to take it for a drive? Clearly. But how could I have guessed that my car and all of my money would end up at the bottom of a mountain pass?

What was I supposed to do now? I had no car, I had no cash, and if I wasn't mistaken, Dr. Sonya had someone else scheduled to check into my room tonight.

It wasn't like I didn't have any options. If worst came to worst, I could always use my credit card or call home. But I didn't want to do that. For once in my life, I wanted to show my father that I wasn't completely helpless. I could take care of myself. But the more time that passed on my little adventure, the more I started to think that I couldn't.

Entering the bed-and-breakfast, the faces of four people immediately turned towards me. They looked like two sets of couples dressed for an adventure vacation. Wearing hiking boots and with large backpacks on the floor next to the couch, I reasoned that these were the visitors that Dr. Sonya had said would be replacing me. I wasn't sure what to say to them, so instead of saying anything, I hurried past them to my room.

Behind my locked door, I collapsed onto the bed and stared at the ceiling. I felt so lost. I had to do something, didn't I? I couldn't just lay here hoping everything would workout. Didn't self-reliant people take action? Didn't they anticipate what would happen next and prepare for it?

Paralyzed, I laid there for more than an hour considering what I should do. I knew that Dillon would help me if he could, but that wasn't our relationship. I was the one who had adopted him. Dillon had been the son of my favorite housekeeper. After my parents arranged a play date, I decided that he would get the life I wished I had.

When he graduated from high school, I convinced my father to start a scholarship program and then made sure that he got it. I also made sure that his dorm room at college was furnished with everything he would need. The scholarship included spending money so he didn't have to get a job, and he got a clothing allowance so he could find a great guy and have a happy life.

I didn't do this because I wanted anything from him. He is my friend. I just want him to be happy. I'm sure that he would help me now if he could. But he was in New Jersey, and I knew the exact amount in his bank account. Asking Dillon for help wasn't an option.

Hearing a knock on the door I snapped out of my downward spiral. Quickly pulling myself together, I sat up. It had gotten dark since I had laid down. Scrambling to my feet, I flicked on a light.

"Yes?" I said, suddenly face to face with Cali's chiseled cheekbones.

"I was wondering if you're gonna be checking out soon?" he said with an unmistakable weight on his shoulders.

I didn't want to burden him with my trivial problems. He had enough to deal with thanks to me.

"Yes. Of course. I guess I just lost track of time."

"It's just that there's someone scheduled for this room, and I still have to clean it…"

"I understand."

"If you need more time…"

"No. I don't have much. I can be out in a few minutes."

Instead of replying, his gaze rolled over me. It gave me a warm feeling that settled deep inside of me.

Tightening his lips, he gave me a nod and returned downstairs.

Well, this was it. I was going to have to make a decision. Tossing the few things I had into my bag, I took a last look at myself in the mirror and left the room.

"I'm out," I told Cali when I found him in the kitchen."

"Okay, thanks," he said, scurrying up to the room behind me.

With nowhere to go, I joined the guests in the living room. It was a comfortable space. The furniture had pictures of birds on the upholstery. There was an ornately designed throw rug under the coffee table in front of it and shelves surrounding the space with books and knickknacks from around the world.

I wondered how it was to grow up in a place like this. It felt like a home filled with love. I knew what that was like. My father was intensely devoted to his family. My mother, my brother, and I were everything to him. It was the rest of the world that had a reason to fear him.

It only took twenty minutes for Cali to return and escort the new guests to their rooms. He looked at me and our eyes made contact for a moment. But that was it. He was busy. I understood. How was he supposed to know what I was going through? Besides, he had real things to worry about.

Thirty minutes later, when he returned to the living room and found that I hadn't moved, I felt embarrassed. I couldn't look at him.

"Is everything okay?" he asked me, drawing my eyes to his.

Staring at him, tears welled in my eyes. I was being ridiculous. I knew it. I had options. I had nothing to complain about. But here I was crying while a person who could be losing his mother remained strong.

"I'm sorry. I'll get out of your hair now," I said getting up, grabbing my bag, and hurrying to the door.

"Wait. Stop!" he ordered, halting me. Facing away, I couldn't look at him.

"You don't have a car. Where are you going?"

"I can call for a ride."

"If you could do that, you would have already. Do you have anywhere to go?"

"Really, you don't have to worry about me. How's your mother?"

When he didn't answer, I turned to face him. Pain rippled through him.

"The doctor says that she'll eventually be alright. But I could barely stand to see her like that. She's always been so full of life, ya know. To see her lying there with tubes attached to her, I couldn't take it."

Without thinking, I rushed to him and gripped his shoulder. If I had thought before I did it, I might not have. When he didn't pull away, I was glad I had.

"The doctor says she's gonna be alright?"

He nodded confirmation.

"That's really good. I can't tell you how happy I am to hear that."

As if regretting he had given me a peak under his mask, he quickly straightened up and pulled away.

"Thank you. And, I'm so sorry about what happened to your car. My mother has insurance. It will take care of it."

"Seriously, don't worry about it. You just worry about your mother and everything else I'm sure you have going on."

"I'll be fine. But you didn't answer my question. Do you have anywhere to go?"

I wondered what I should tell him. I had already said that I would be fine. He hadn't accepted that answer. Deciding I should tell him the truth, I shook my head, no.

"Then, you'll stay here," he said kindly.

"But the room is gone."

"You'll stay in my room," he said confidently.

My mouth dropped open as I stared at him wondering what he was suggesting. He quickly clarified.

"I'll stay in my mother's room. My room isn't much but…"

"No, thank you. I'm sure it'll be more than enough," I said as relief washed through me.

"You'll need to give me a few minutes to straighten it up and maybe change the sheets," he said with his fair-skinned cheeks turning red.

"Don't go through any trouble." I implored.

"No, just give me a minute. I'll be right back," he said hurrying up the stairs.

I watched his ass as he left. Damn!

Chapter 2

Cali

As I led him down the hallway to my bedroom, I pictured the guy following me. His tousled, curly hair fell halfway down his forehead. And his wide eyes and full pink lips reminded me of a Kewpie doll. He had to be the hottest guy I had ever met.

This was not the time to think about that, though. I had other things to worry about. My mother was in the hospital. It was hard not to blame myself for her being there.

Ever since I learned that Titus, Claude, and I were brothers, things had been tense between my mother and I. When I had confronted her with it, she had tightened her lips and walked away. She knew. For my entire life, she knew that I had brothers and hadn't told me. Why? How could she do that to me?

"Here it is," I said, turning back to the shorter, lean guy behind me.

"Are you sure this is okay?" he asked, his eyes hinting to his vulnerability.

"It's no problem," I said, staring at him blankly.

The gorgeous guy continued to look at me as if there was something he wanted to say. I couldn't imagine what it would be. Staring back, I had an ache in my chest. Overwhelmed by a desire to pull him into my arms and slip my fingers into his nest of hair, I looked away to gather myself.

"Do you think your mother will be coming home soon?" he asked, drawing my gaze.

"Don't worry. You can have the room for as long as you need it."

Hil looked embarrassed.

"That wasn't why I was asking."

Staring at him again, it was clear that that wasn't what he was asking.

"Right. No, I'm sure it will be at least a couple of days. The doctor told me that she looks a lot worse than she is. Luckily, it's mostly scratches and bruises. She escaped a lot of the internal damage that might have made things tricky. But she's not completely out of the woods. I'll be heading back in the morning to check on her," I said, again being overcome by regret.

"Please, give her my best."

I stared at him. The pain in his eyes told me that he really did think that what happened to my mother was his fault. I couldn't understand why. He wasn't the one who had crashed into her or had left the scene of the crime. He was the one who called the ambulance that rescued her.

I tightened my lips and nodded before turning toward my mother's bedroom and leaving Hil in my wake. Opening the door at the end of the hall, I didn't look back. I desperately wanted to, but I didn't want to get too attached. He could be gone by the time I woke up and I was tired of having my heart broken.

Trust was an issue for me and it didn't help that the person I thought I could trust the most had allowed me to live a lie. So I wasn't going to let myself feel something for Hil no matter how gorgeous his eyes were. I had to protect myself from him.

But with the door locked behind me, I pictured him again. As soon as I did, my cock got hard. I placed my hand on it and squeezed.

This wasn't the first time I had had feelings for a guy, but the other times hadn't felt like this. I had had crushes, but this felt like more. And the more I felt, the more I knew I needed to fight it.

Trying to shake it from my mind, I stripped off my shirt and jeans and fell into my mother's bed. It was weird being here. I hadn't slept in it since I was a kid.

What I had told Hil was true. Dr. Tom, my mother's doctor, had said that he thought my mother would fully recover. But what I hadn't told Hil was how awful she looked. Purple bruises covered her fair skin.

And pumped with painkillers, she stared at me as if I wasn't there.

My mother had always been so strong. So full of life. I used to think of her has being "too much". Now I would give anything to have her back to the way she was.

There had to be a reason she hadn't told me that I had brothers, right? And why she had always refused to tell me anything about my father? There had to be.

But none of that was important now. The only thing that mattered was that she got better. And I was going to do whatever I had to to make that happen.

Sitting in the waiting room the next morning, images danced through my mind. Would Mama look better? Worse? Were the drugs that she was on masking a head injury that would rob her of her spirit?

I barely slept the night before thinking about it. I had been a fool to fight with her. I would now give anything to take it back.

"Mr. Shearer?" the stout, dark-skinned woman said from behind the receptionist desk.

Getting up, I quickly stood in front of her.

"That's me," I said with my heart thumping in my throat.

"You can go back now," she said, barely looking at me.

Was her uneasy eye contact because things had not gone well overnight? Heat washed through me considering the possibility.

"She was moved to room 201. That's on the second floor. Would you like directions?"

"You changed her room?"

The woman's tired eyes met mine. After only a second, they popped back down to the sheet in front of her.

"It says here that she was moved due to an upgrade in her status. It's a good thing," she said with a practiced smile.

"Thank you," I said relieved and headed towards the stairs.

I didn't like the smell of hospitals. It smelled like death. I knew that too well. I couldn't take losing my mother. And as much as I tried not to think about it, the thought flooded my mind as I crossed the halls.

When I found room 201, I reached for the knob and paused. I really couldn't take it if Mama's condition had taken a turn for the worse. This whole thing was a nightmare. My heart raced and my breath labored thinking about it.

Gathering up as much courage as I could, I knocked and pressed lightly on the door. Peeking in, I held my breath.

"Cali?" a strained but familiar voice said from within.

"Yeah, it's me, Mama."

"I'm glad to see you," she said with drowsy eyes and a smile.

Allowing the door to close behind me, I moved to the side of her bed. Although she was more awake than she had been the night before, she might have looked worse. All of her purple bruises had darkened. I couldn't imagine that being a good sign, but hadn't they moved her to a new room because she was doing better?

"That bad, huh?" my mother said, reading the look on my face.

"No, Mama. You're looking better."

My mother smiled. "Here's a secret, Cali. You have a tell when you lie. A mother knows," she said emphasizing her usually light Jamaican accent.

Was that true? Could she tell when I was lying? I was certainly lying this time.

"Mama, how did this happen?"

Sadness entered my mother's eyes. It was the same one she got whenever I brought up my newly-found brothers.

"Does this have something to do with my father?"

She looked at me, staring into my eyes.

"It does, doesn't it?"

"I don't know that. And neither could you, so there's no point in asking about it."

"What are you talking about? Someone told me that your car was rear-ended. You could have been killed. I almost lost you. If you're still in danger, I need to know about it. If someone's trying to hurt you because of me…"

Mama took my hand in hers. Looking at her, all I could see were the tubes attached to her arms.

"What happened was an accident. That's all it was."

"But what if it wasn't? You have to tell me who my father is. If he's someone dangerous, I have to know. Titus, Claude, and I need to know."

For the first time since finding out there was more to my past than I was being told, my mother looked at me with empathy. I hoped it would be followed by an explanation. It wasn't.

"Even now you're not going to say anything?"

"Cali, there is nothing to say."

As relieved as I was that my mother seemed more like herself, I was once again furious at her. I deserved to know the truth. She was withholding a part of who I was from me.

Maybe if I knew who my father was, it would explain things about me that I didn't understand. I wanted to yell that at my mother, but I couldn't. Not now, and maybe never again.

"I'm going to be taking a break from school to take care of the bed-and-breakfast," I said to her, changing the topic.

"No!" she replied emphatically.

"What do you mean no? There are guests staying there. Now that business is starting to pick up, we have to think about reviews."

"Promise me that this won't affect your schoolwork."

"Do you think I care about school right now? Do you see where you are?"

"Promise me!"

"Mama!"

"I said, promise me! Your education is what's important. That should always come first."

"There is nothing more important than getting you healthy," I explained to her.

She squeezed my hand. "Thank you. But the doctors here will take care of that. You just worry about your grades. Let me worry about the business."

"You say that, but what could you do from this bed?"

"More than you think," she said with a smile.

I looked down at my mother who was covered in bruises but still thought that she could do it all. That was the woman I had grown up with. Not even driving into a forty-foot-deep ravine could stop her. I smiled and conceded.

"I'll stay in school. But I'll have to take a break, at least for a few days."

"No, you won't."

"Mama, you're being ridiculous."

"Promise me," she said softly but with more weight than any two words deserve to have.

"I promise," I told her, knowing that she was the master of doing the impossible. Now I was going to have to figure out how to do the same.

Chapter 3

Hil

"Okay, Hil. You have to tell me where you are," Dillon said, using the tone he implored whenever he wanted to be taken seriously.

"I told you, I'm fine," I said, looking around Cali's football-themed room.

"You say that, but how do I know it's true? This is coming from the person who said they might be unavailable for a few days and then fell off the grid for more than a week. Does that sound like someone whose word I can count on?"

As much as I didn't want to admit it, Dillon was right. It was a shitty thing for me to have done. I just took off without telling anyone where I was going or when I would be back.

I didn't regret doing it because it was the only way I could get out. And what if my father, or even my brother contacted him. Dillon was a really bad liar. If he knew, they would know he knew and eventually get it out of him.

I was keeping Dillon safe by not telling him that I was going… even if it killed me that he no longer felt that he could trust me… and Dillon's trust meant everything to me…

"Fine," I said crumbling under the thought that I could lose him as a friend. "I'll tell you where I am. But no specifics."

"You know me, I'll take what I can get," Dillon said, jokingly referring to his love life.

I laughed.

"I'm currently in a hot football player's bedroom while lying snuggly beneath his sheets."

There was a pause on the other end followed by a piercing, "What?"

I couldn't stop the smile that plastered across my face.

"Yeah. I'm staring at all of his football equipment right now," I said, looking at the sports gear that had been piled in the corner of the room.

"Oh, now you have to tell me where you are."

"I told you, I'm fine."

"Um, you sound a little better than just fine."

"Maybe," I said with a smile.

"But I don't understand. Yesterday you told me you thought you killed somebody."

Remembering how it felt waiting in the hospital for Cali wiped the smile from my face.

"Yeah. That happened too."

"How did you almost kill someone?" Dillon asked delicately.

"I should have gotten rid of my family's car as soon as I passed the first car rental place."

"By the way, Hil, when did get your driver's license?"

Dillon knew the answer to that question. I hadn't. Not only did we both grow up in New York City, but I had a driver to take me anywhere I needed to go. When we arrived, my driver turned into my bodyguard. That had been no way to grow up.

Although, to be fair, it took less than two weeks of being on my own for someone to run my car off the road. Was I making a horrible mistake not having protection? Was I signing my own death certificate by running from the people who were paid to keep me safe?

I didn't want to think about that, right now. I had gotten out and I wanted to make the best of it. I needed to figure out how to have a life.

Remy had one, and as my father's first born, he was in a lot more danger than I was. Yet, my father didn't require him to have a bodyguard. He could do whatever he wanted. It was only me who he thought couldn't take care of myself. I had to prove him wrong. I had to show him that I could make it on my own.

"Has Remy asked about me again?"

"Since the last time I spoke to you?"

"Remy can be persistent."

Dillon laughed. "I wish. I don't know if you know this, but your brother is hot. He could slide into my DM's anytime and have whatever he wants."

"And that's why I can't tell you where I am," I said disappointed. "Also, ew."

Dillon didn't respond.

I had always been insecure when it came to Remy. He and I were nothing alike. Not only did he get all the height, he also got all the muscles and tattoos. I was just his soft, little brother that needed someone to do everything for him. I hated it. I would do anything for that not to be true.

"I'm gonna go," I told Dillon, losing my enthusiasm for the call.

"Go and do what?" he asked, prying me for more.

"To be honest, I don't know. I'm pretty much stuck here for now. Maybe have breakfast. I'll figure things out from there."

"I want you to call me every day to let me know you're okay. If you don't want me to tell Remy that I heard from you, you're gonna have to give me that."

"I'll call you," I told him, hiding how much it meant to me that he cared.

"And you know you're gonna have to give me more details about the football player, right?"

I smiled.

"As soon as I have something to share, believe me, you'll be the first person I tell."

"Stay safe," he said with enough sincerity to tell me how worried he actually was for me.

"I promise," I said, ending the call and looking around.

What was I going to do today? The previous few days I had driven around to the hiking spots Dr. Sonya had told me about. I didn't actually go on the hikes. That would have been crazy. But the views from the trailheads were beautiful.

That, however, was back when I had a car. I was going to have to do something about that. But what? The only money I had were the few hundred dollars I had in my wallet. That wasn't going to get me very far.

I didn't see any way this could end without me crawling back to my family admitting that I had failed. That might have been inevitable, but it didn't have to happen today. What did have to happen was breakfast. Hopefully it was going to be waiting for me when I got downstairs.

Pulling myself together for when I ran into the gorgeous guy who had slept a few doors down, I left my room and headed for the kitchen. Crossing the living room, I saw the same pair of couples that had been there when I had gotten back from the hospital.

"Excuse me, you're staying here as well, right?" the skinny, grizzly looking man in flannel and hiking boots asked me.

"Yes, you checked in last night, right?"

"Yeah. Do you know if there's supposed to be breakfast?" he asked, flashing a realization through my mind.

The gorgeous guy had said that he was heading to the hospital early. Considering he was going there to see his mother, and his mother was the one to make breakfast, the kitchen was going to be empty.

"Yes, there is. And it's usually great. But…" My eyes darted around as I figured out what I should say.

"But?" the guy echoed.

I looked at him with an idea.

"But it might be a little limited this morning. Can you give me a second? I'll go check on it," I told him, excited by my idea.

Leaving the group, I entered the kitchen. Looking around, nothing seemed too intimidating. Hadn't I watched our chef cook for us a thousand times? Some of what I saw had to have rubbed off on me, didn't it? How hard could making breakfast be?

Opening the well-stocked fridge, I stared inside. Everything was in there. It looked like enough food to feed an army. It was overwhelming.

"Eggs," I said remembering the delicious scramble Dr. Sonya had made for me the morning before.

Retrieving one of them, I stared at it and then pulled out another. These were definitely eggs. There was no doubt about it. And somehow what was inside was supposed to be cooked and place on a plate with a garnish on the side.

What was I doing? I didn't know how to scramble eggs. I couldn't even boil an egg. If I was left in a fully stocked kitchen by myself for a week, I would probably starve to death.

"Do you know if it will be ready soon?" the scruffy guy asked, poking his head past the kitchen door. "We have a hiking tour scheduled in an hour. We're wondering if we should instead grab breakfast at the diner down the street."

"No, you don't have to go anywhere else. Breakfast will be coming up in a second. I'll let you know when it's ready," I said, hiding my terror with a smile. I was sure he didn't notice.

When he retreated with a doubtful look, I turned back to the impossible task in front of me and tried not to panic.

Closing my eyes and taking a deep breath, I settled myself.

"You can do this, Hil. It doesn't have to be fancy. It just has to be something that qualifies as breakfast."

With a new mission, I returned the eggs to their container in the fridge. Scrambled eggs were intermediate. I was a beginner. So I looked around for something that was beginner level.

On the back of the top shelf were a few of Marcus's pastries.

"A continental breakfast?" I contemplated, remembering a few of my family's trips to France.

Retrieving the croissants, I opened every cabinet until I found plates. Arranging them as nicely as I could, I next looked for a knife and the clay butter container Dr. Sonya had presented to me the last few mornings.

"There it is," I said as relief filled me.

This was close, but I needed something else.

"Cereal!" I blurted, not knowing why I hadn't thought of it before.

Scouring the cupboards, I found two boxes of cereal. I would offer the group both. Retrieving bowls and the milk, I took it past the swinging door to the dining room table and laid it all out. Returning with the croissants a few seconds later, I called the group into the dining area and nervously watched their faces.

They didn't look too disappointed. Shouldn't I take that as a win? I mean, I had figured out how to feed four people. I could technically be considered a sustainer of life.

"Thank you," the group leader said before they all sat down and dug in.

Struggling to contain my excitement, I said, "Just let me know if you need anything else," and then retreated to the kitchen.

It's hard for me to express how great I felt having taken care of this. Maybe I wasn't as helpless as everyone thought. Perhaps I could do this. It wasn't like everyone else was smarter than me. It was just that no one had ever given me the opportunity. I had never had to. But if I did, might I rise to the occasion?

Waiting in the kitchen for the couples to leave, I reentered the dining area with a plan. The excitement of it made me tingle. It would be something that I couldn't even imagine myself doing just days earlier. But I was sure I could do this.

Retrieving the plates and extra food, I put everything away and placed the dishes in the sink. Looking around to see what else I could do, I realized that the dishes weren't going to wash themselves. The question was, though, how do you wash dishes?

Looking around, I spotted a bottle of dish soap. Wondering how it worked, I squeezed some of it onto the bowls. The florescent green lines just laid there. I wasn't sure what I was expecting it to do.

Finding a sponge at the back of the sink, I came up with a new plan. It was just like taking a bath, right? Except with dishes? There wasn't more to it than that. Right?

When that was done, I placed them in the draining rack and looked down at them pleased. I had just washed my first set of dishes. It really wasn't that hard. More than that, I had a sense of accomplishment that I rarely felt. I really was capable of more than anyone gave me credit for.

With a newfound excitement, I left the kitchen for my room. I had to figure out what else I could do. There had to be something, right? It was then that I thought of Dillon. His mother had been our housekeeper. If there was anyone who would know, it would to be him.

"How does someone run a bed-and-breakfast?" I asked my friend.

"How am I supposed to know that? I've never even been to a bed-and-breakfast. Have you forgotten that I've never been further than New Jersey?"

"I know," I said feeling bad about assuming. "It's just that…"

"… my mother is a housekeeper?"

"No!"

"Seriously, Hil?"

"Okay. Is that bad?"

"It's not great."

"Sorry."

"No, that's fine. I guess I'm just being sensitive. Everyone at this school acts like they have money to burn. They keep inviting me to things that there's no way I can afford."

"If you need me to send you more money…" I told him feeling bad.

"That's not why I said that, Hil. Please, just be my best friend right now."

I swallowed, unsure of how many things I had said poorly. I wanted to be supportive. And wasn't money the way my parents had shown me that they cared? Wait. Was I just acting like my parents? Yikes!

"You're right, Dillon. And that sucks. But I know you. You're probably the best guy there. You're the best person I know.

"And if I wasn't the only guy you knew, that would mean so much to me, Hil" Dillon said almost sounding sincere.

"Whatever," I said with a laugh. "You know what I mean."

"You mean that you love me. Yes, I understand. And I love you too."

I took a second to think about how lucky I was to have Dillon in my life before my thoughts turned back to my brilliant plan.

"So, do you think your mother would know how to run one?"

As Dillon ran through the list of reasons why he wasn't going to ask her, I came up with a list that answered my own question. Most of them could be summed up in two words: ' be awesome.' How hard could that be?

For the next few hours, I chatted with Dillon. When he hung up to go to class, I walked through the house full of energy. That continued until Cali returned. Hearing the front door open, I rushed downstairs to greet him. He seemed startled by my presence as I descended the stairs. He stared at me with a tortured look. I froze.

"Is your mother alright?" I asked, feeling a sudden lump in my throat.

"She's feeling better, thanks," he said, before passing me as he headed toward the stairs.

"Wait, could I talk to you about something?" I said, grabbing his attention. The way his steely eyes locked on me when he turned made my knees weak.

"What is it?" he said gruffly.

I knew he was having a hard time right now, so I tried not to take it personally. But it also made me think about what he would look like if he smiled.

Catching himself, he hung his head with an apologetic look.

"I'm sorry. I just have a lot on my mind."

"That's perfectly fine. You have a lot to worry about. Which is kind of what I wanted to talk to you about."

He turned, looking at me questioningly. I felt the heat from his gaze. It was enough to make me think naughty thoughts about him. Pushing those aside for the time being, I took a breath, gathered myself and then asked him to follow me.

Taking him into the kitchen, I showed him the dishes I had cleaned.

"So, this morning the other guests asked about breakfast."

"Oh, shit!"

"That's okay. I took care of it."

"You took care of it?"

I smiled. "Yeah. I offered them a few of the croissants in the fridge and cereal. I know it wasn't what your mother usually prepares, but they seemed happy with it. And it was something you didn't have to worry about."

Cali looked at me, not saying a word.

"Was that okay?"

"Yes, of course. I'm just sorry you had to do it. That was my responsibility."

"Don't worry about it. In fact, I was thinking that I could help you out more. I mean, until your mother gets back. But, even then, I'm sure there are things that you'll need help with," I said, trying to hide my vulnerability.

Cali just stared at me. I melted under his gaze. What was he thinking? Did he see me the way everyone else did? Incapable of taking care of myself, much less anything as complicated as this place? I was about to retract my offer when he relieved me of my suffering.

"Have you ever worked at a bed-and-breakfast before?"

"No, but I have a lot of experience watching people work at a bed-and-breakfast," I offered, knowing it wasn't nearly the same thing.

The gorgeous, built guy continued to stare at me. The longer he did, the more naked I felt. I couldn't take it anymore. "Please say something."

"I'm sorry," he said with sincerity. "I was just thinking of something my mother said."

"What was that?"

"It doesn't matter. Do you know what's involved with taking care of a place like this?"

"No. But I can learn," I told him enthusiastically.

"There are a lot of things that aren't fun to do," he explained.

"So, I'm sure you would prefer to find someone else to do them."

"Are you sure you're up for it? You don't strike me as someone who likes to get their hands dirty."

"I can get my hands dirty. My whole life everyone's assumed that I'm helpless. It's not true. I can do stuff. Someone just needs to give me a chance. If you let me help you, I promise you won't regret it. Besides, I owe you this."

"Why do you owe me?"

I apologized, reconsidering what I said. I couldn't tell him that the reason his mother was in the hospital was because of me. I didn't know much, but I knew that wasn't something that you said in a job interview.

"It was my car your mother had the accident in."

"Which is why, if anything, I owe you."

I smiled.

"Then, if you do owe me, you can pay me back by letting me help you," I said beaming about how clever I was. "I mean, you kind of owe me at least that, don't you?"

Cali cracked a smile. It was his first. It sent a rush through me that made my balls tingle.

"I guess I do."

"Does that mean you'll let me help you?"

"It's the least I can do."

Feeling over the moon, I caught myself before I got too excited.

"Umm, here is probably where I should tell you that I don't really have any experience with stuff."

"When you say 'stuff,' what are you referring to?"

"Bed-and-breakfast stuff. Life stuff. Really, you could just take your pick."

I was expecting him to look at me like the pathetic loser that I was. But he didn't. It was almost like he felt sorry for me, but not in a pathetic way. With one look, he seemed to tell me that he would take care of me. I had to be looking way too much into it, but it made me feel good.

"I can teach you," he conceded.

"I swear I'll be the best student. What will it be first, Teach?"

"We could start with how to wash dishes," he said, confusing me.

"What do you mean? That's the one thing I figured out how to do," I said, pointing at the dishes in the drainer.

"His eyes bounced to the dishes and then back towards me.

"What?" I asked when he didn't say anything.

"You did a great job. Although, you might have missed a spot or two."

I turned back towards the dishes again. I didn't know what he was talking about until I inspected them closer. It was like, until that very moment, the spots were invisible. It had to be some sort of crazy dishwashing magic.

"Oh!" I said, turning to him embarrassed.

He chuckled, seemingly amused.

Chapter 4

Cali

Staring into Hil's large brown eyes, I wondered what I had gotten myself into. He did something to me. Standing as close to him as I was, all I could think about was pushing my fingers through his large curls, wrapping my other hand around his small waist and kissing him hard.

Should I be thinking about a guy like him at a time like this? Probably not. But I couldn't help it. From the moment I saw him standing next to Marcus at the hospital, I lost a little of myself.

Titus and I had spoken a lot since finding out we were brothers. Much of it was about how he felt finally dating the guy he had been in love with for so long. He told me that from the moment he met Lou, it felt different. He was right.

I could barely explain how what I felt for this stranger differed from the crushes I've had in the past, but it was there. Staring at Hil that first time felt like standing in the path of a tidal wave. I felt the crash building in front of me. In my next breath, I was gone.

"We can start with cooking lessons in the morning, if that's okay with you," I said after showing him how I usually clean the dishes.

"If you want, we can start right now," he said enthusiastically.

One of the things I had noticed about him in our few interactions was how quickly he switched to being upbeat. Yes, he was respectful at the hospital. And, he was weighed down last night. But given the briefest bit of positivity, he glowed.

Why was that? It must have been nice having such an easy life. Did he grow up having anything to complain about? I certainly didn't know what that was like.

"We should start in the morning. I'll show you how to make breakfast before I drive back to campus."

"That would be fantastic," he sighed with a smile that lit up the room.

Unsure what to do, I stared struggling to take my eyes off of him. When the silence drew out, he spoke.

"Have you eaten yet?"

"What time is it?"

"Almost dinner time," he suggested vulnerably.

I looked at him not sure what he was suggesting.

"I can cook something up if you're hungry."

"Actually, I was thinking I could take you out. We could go to that diner down the street. It's the least I can do considering you're letting me stay here for free."

"You thought you were staying here for free?" I asked, only holding the joke for a second. His face turned fifty shades of pink before I said, "I'm joking. You're welcome to stay here as long as you need to. In fact, I'm hoping you do."

"Oh, okay," he said with relief. "In that case, allow me to take you to dinner."

I looked at him again. How long could I sit across from his full pink lips without wanting to press mine against them?

"Maybe I shouldn't."

Disappointment flashed across Hil's face. "Why not?"

"There are things that you don't know about me. I could be dangerous."

Hil smiled. "Maybe I'm dangerous too. It sounds like we're a perfect match" he said with a flirtatious glint in his eye.

Feeling his response, blood rushed to my cock. Could I spend time with this guy and not fall for him? I had a lot going on. My mother had made me promise to keep going to school while running the business and taking care of her. But, hadn't he just offered me the perfect solution? Didn't I at least owe him dinner?

"Yeah. Dinner would be great. Thank you," I said, staring into his eyes and feeling a warm wave wash through me.

His excitement to spend time with me was more than I was ready for. It felt good. I was going to have to watch myself to make sure I didn't let things get out of control.

Leaving him to clean up and clear my thoughts, I returned downstairs to find him on the couch. He sprung up when he saw me.

"Are you ready?" he said with a beaming smile.

I offered a half-hearted smile in return. He was being nothing but nice, and everything about him made me want to know more. But was I ready for anything like that? I had long accepted that I liked guys, but here was one who liked me back. That made things a hell of a lot more real.

With him following me to my truck, we got in and pulled off. Peeking over, I saw him staring at me with a smile. Why was he doing that? What was he thinking? I wanted to know everything about him. What was going on with me?

After only a few minutes, I pulled into the parking lot of the diner and scanned the trucks to see who was there. Titus and most of my friends were back at school. It's where I should have been, considering I had a class before noon tomorrow. My other brother

Claude, who had moved back to town after graduating the previous semester, wasn't here either.

I wasn't sure why I was concerned about who would see Hil and me together. There were enough same sex couples in town to make it a common thing. And it wasn't like I kept my attraction for guys a secret. I don't know what it was. Maybe there was just a part of me that wanted to keep Hil for myself.

"I can't tell you how much I like this diner," Hil said, breaking the silence.

"You clearly don't get out much," I joked.

"I really don't. I mean, I've traveled a lot with my family. But when it comes to going to places to have fun, I couldn't tell you what it's like."

"How is that?"

"How is it that I don't get out much?"

"Yeah. How is it that you could travel but not get out?"

It already felt like I had asked Hil more questions than I had anybody in my life.

"My family travels a lot for business. We go to Europe regularly. My father has family in France. But, when we get back to New York, he prefers to keep me trapped. Before I came here, I was ready to chew my own leg off to get away."

I considered everything he had said. It brought up more questions than answers.

"So, you're from New York?"

"Yep. I live in a place downtown."

"By yourself?"

"Oh, God, no. I wish. But I have a lot of my own space in our apartment. I don't have to see my parents if I don't want to. So, at least there's that. How about you?"

"What about me?"

"You go to school, right?"

"East Tennessee University."

"And you're on the football team?"

I shook my head. "Our season ended a few months ago."

"Did you win the championship," he asked with a devilish smile.

"Yeah."

"Wait, you did? I was just joking about that."

"We're national champions two years running."

"Oh! Wait, are you, like, famous?"

I laughed. "Depends on who you talk to."

"Seriously?"

"I set a few records last year," I confirmed. "People tend to remember your name when you do that."

I wasn't sure why I was telling him that. Usually, I couldn't give a shit about what people thought about me. But I wanted him to like me. I wanted him to be impressed. The look he gave me back was giving me thoughts. I considered what he looked like naked.

He leaned forward, clasping his fingers and allowing me to smell his gentle scent.

"So, tell me something that you don't usually tell people, Mr. Famous Football Player," he asked as if we were on a date.

Were we on a date? Was that what was happening? I wasn't really the dating type. When you're on a team that wins a national championship, you tend to get offered anything you want from anyone you want. But this felt different. Did I want to give him an answer?

We were interrupted by Mike, Titus's soon to be stepfather and the owner of the diner. He looked at Hil as much as I thought he would. Although I knew that Titus's mother was good with him having a boyfriend, I wasn't sure how Mike felt about it. Taking our orders and returning to the kitchen, I didn't have to find out.

"I get lonely a lot," I told Hil when we were again alone.

"What?" he asked confused.

"You asked me to tell you something I don't usually share. That's it."

Hil's expression shifted. Maybe it was empathy. I couldn't be sure. Whatever it was, it made me feel naked in front of him. I don't know why I told him that. I just couldn't stop myself.

"Me too," he said, melting my heart. "I only have one friend. Dillon. And I'm only friends with him because he was my housekeeper's son. He's great. Don't get me wrong. But…"

Hil's eyes dipped in sadness. Everything in me made me want to slide next to him, pull him into my arms, and never let him go. I wanted to protect him, to make him happy. Yet, I didn't move. I just sat there wanting to but not doing anything. What was wrong with me? Why couldn't I just act on how I felt?

Chapter 5

Hil

For a guy who didn't speak much, he certainly said a lot when he did. Dinner with Cali was one of the best conversations I've had in my life. Seriously, Dillon was great. I couldn't imagine my life without him. But there was something missing in our relationship and I'm not talking about sex.

Although, on that topic, I really want to have sex for the first time. More specifically, I want to have it with Cali.

When I met him, all I could think about was what it would feel like wrapped in his arms with his thick manhood inside me. But having gotten to know him, I've realized that there is more to him than his shockingly gorgeous body. We have a connection.

Returning to the bed-and-breakfast after a lot of conversation—by conversation, I mean that I did a lot of talking while he sat there looking angsty and beautiful—he walked me to my room and stared at me. God, did I want to invite him in. But I wasn't even sure if I should. So, instead, I said goodnight and then laid in bed clutching my hard cock, imagining him stripping me naked and having his way with me.

The next morning, I was up at sunrise bubbling with excitement for my first cooking lesson with Cali. Staring at myself in the mirror as I got ready, I wondered what I was excited about. Whether or not he was into guys, there was no way he would be interested in a guy like me. I was awkward and weird, and around him it was like I couldn't figure out what to do with my hands.

I was nothing special, and he was a famous, record-breaking football player who was lip-bitingly hot. I was fooling myself.

It wasn't going to stop me, though. I couldn't shut down what I was feeling for him if I tried. It was like he had his hooks in me. I was at his mercy. And considering the painful broken heart that would follow when I fell back to earth, my chest clenched.

Washing the thought out of my mind, I turned my focus to what I was about to do. Cali had said that he would be leaving early to get back to campus in time for class. But before he did, he would teach me the magic of scrambling eggs.

Considering how much I was looking forward to it, I wondered why I hadn't asked someone to teach me how to cook before. I had plenty of chances. My father always hired the best chefs.

I guess there was something special about Cali teaching me. I didn't know much about dating, but hadn't I seen a movie where a couple fell in love taking a cooking class together? Would our meet cute be when our hands touched as we both reached for the salt? There was salt in scrambled eggs, right?

Either way, I would soon learn. And with him behind me as I cracked eggs into the pan, he'll wrap his muscular arms around me, take my chin in his hand, and kiss my neck.

I wonder what would his hard cock will feel like pressed against my ass? I struggled to breathe as I thought about it. And when my cock fought against the zipper of my jeans, I pushed it against my body enjoying the pleasure that followed.

Pulling myself together and waiting for my erection to die down, I finished getting dressed and scurried downstairs. To my surprise, he was waiting for me in the kitchen.

"Am I late? When do you have to leave?"

"We have an hour. That should be plenty of time," he said without the soft vulnerability that he had shown the night before. He was back to being Mr. Serious. Mr., *I have the weight of the world on my shoulders*. I wondered if he would want me to give him a massage.

"Are you ready to begin?" he asked me before my erection had a chance to return.

"I was born ready for this," I told him, throwing my hands into the air like a boxer.

For the next thirty minutes, he explained how to scramble an egg. He clearly didn't know what he was up against.

"So, you just take an egg and crack it into a bowl," he explained.

"Wait. Does the size of the bowl matter? How do you crack an egg? Are there supposed to be so many shells in it? What if you can't get all of the shells out? How many shells can you eat before you taste more shell than egg?"

Like I said, he had no idea.

He then explained what type of eggs you could use, what type of pans, how much a pinch of salt was, and how much butter to use. After that he explained what was considered butter and why he thought I could do this. In the end, it tasted fairly good.

"Now, it's your turn," he said, threatening to poison us both.

"I'm not sure if I'm ready to do it by myself. Maybe you should show me one more time," I suggested, my hands sweating.

"You can do this. Really, you can. The great thing about cooking is that you get a lot of chances to get it right. You can always add more salt, more butter. You don't have to be perfect your first time out. Just take your time and do your best."

I stared at Cali. I had never heard someone say that before. There wasn't a lot of room for errors in my household. I was a Lyon. We weren't supposed to make mistakes.

My brother, Remy, was perfect at everything. I was the only one who was too much of a screw up to take care of myself.

"Come on. You can do this. If you get it wrong, we'll do it again tomorrow."

"Are you trying to get me to mess up on purpose?"

That got Mr. Grumpy to crack a smile. I liked to see him smile. It sent a tingle through my body when he did.

"We can do this every morning. As long as it takes," he confirmed with mischief in his eyes.

"In that case…" I said, before grabbing the ingredients and whipping it all together.

I have to admit, what I made didn't taste half bad. It didn't taste like the eggs his mother had made. But it would sustain life.

"Do you know how to make waffles?" I asked him as we sat enjoying our spoils together.

"Why?"

"They're my favorite breakfast food. It might be cool to know how to make them."

"Then, that will be tomorrow's lesson."

"Seriously?" I said, more excited than I should have been.

"I told you, as long as it takes," he said with a glint in his eye that made me hard again. Eventually, I was going to have to do something about that. Maybe he would help me with that too.

Promising to drive back after he was done with classes, Cali left for the day. While he was gone, I cleaned the dishes. That might not have seemed like much, but I actually cleaned them this time so it took awhile. After that, I got adventurous. I waited for the guests to leave their room and then I went in and made their bed.

Did I know how to make a bed? No. But the internet did. Soon, so did I.

I'm still not sure how the woman on the Happy Housekeeping video got the sheets so tight. But, baby steps. And, look at me. I was really doing this.

When Marcus arrived explaining that Tuesdays and Thursdays were the days that Dr. Sonya sold his pastries using the back deck as a makeshift coffee shop, I was thrown for a loop. When I woke up this morning, I didn't know how to scramble eggs. There was no way I could handle coffee.

Luckily, Marcus didn't expect me to. He took care of everything while I sat watching him. The things he did with dough made my feeble attempt at breakfast look like child's play. I had never realized how many levels there were to cooking. I'd always just shown up and ate what was in front of me. How much of life had I been missing?

"So, is Cali dating anyone?" I asked Marcus, trying to sound casual.

"It's hard to tell with him. He doesn't talk much. At least, not to me. But I don't think so."

"Has he ever dated anyone?"

Marcus turned to me. He saw right through my lame questions.

"I wouldn't describe Cali as the sharing type. He was a year behind me at school, but everyone knew him. The girls would talk about him endlessly. They just love the quiet, brooding type."

"And the guys?"

When Marcus stared at me, I could feel my cheeks heating up.

"I don't know. The guys were the guys."

"Meaning?"

"Meaning, he was on the football team. Who doesn't like football players, right?"

I stared at Marcus trying to figure out what he was trying to tell me.

"What about you?"

"What about me?"

"How did you feel about Cali?"

"I told you. We got along fine."

"So, nothing ever happened between you two?"

"Between us?" he laughed. "No. Even if he was into guys, which to be honest, I doubt, I wouldn't be his type."

"Why do you say that?"

Marcus looked away in thought.

"I don't think he likes me very much."

"Who does he like?"

Marcus turned back towards me with the realization of what I was asking.

"You know what? I don't know. I guess he likes Titus. They were roommates before finding out they were brothers. There might have been a few guys on the football team that he liked. But, for the most part, he pretty much keeps to himself."

"So, what you're saying is that he's a real mystery?"

"It's more like he's a tough nut to crack."

I considered everything Marcus told me about Cali and spent the rest of the day wondering if, with him, I was seeing things that weren't there. Marcus had said that he doubted Cali was into guys. He could have been wrong.

On the other hand, hadn't he known Cali his whole life? Yeah, I understood that there were people who were a lot better than at hiding it than I was. But Marcus was putting out serious gay vibes. Although I couldn't, shouldn't he have been able to pick up on something by now?

Thinking about it anxiously until Cali arrived, I looked at him differently as he stepped through the door.

"What?" he asked me when I didn't say anything.

"Just thinking."

"About what?"

"About you… And what you're going to teach me how to cook next," I said, not ready to commit to the truth.

"What about how to make dinner?"

I hesitated. "I don't know, that seems like a lot. Do you remember when I asked you to explain how to boil an egg?"

Cali chuckled. "It's burned into my memory. Trust me, it'll be easy. I'll show you how."

It turns out it was easy…to watch. There were still so many things I didn't know. There seemed to be an instinct about how much of each ingredient to add that Cali couldn't give me a clear answer on.

"So, how much paprika are you sprinkling in?"

"I don't know. Until it smells right."

"How much of the mixed vegetables do you pour in to the pot?"

"A third of the way. Sometimes a half."

"The size of the pot doesn't matter?"

Like I said, he was not prepared for someone like me.

To his credit, every time I asked a question, he thoughtfully answered. It made learning incredibly less stressful. My father once taught me how to spot a counterfeit hundred-dollar bill. It was the last thing he ever tried to teach me. With Cali it felt nothing like that.

Although the two of us sat and talked for longer than we intended—again, with me doing all the talking—we weren't there for too long before Cali apologized and announced that he was heading up to bed.

"It's been a long day. I stopped by the hospital before I came home. Seeing my mother like that takes a lot out of me."

"No, I understand. You should rest. And if you think you won't be able to teach me how to make waffles in the morning, don't worry about it."

"Are you kidding? That's gonna be the highlight of my day," he said, turning me into a puddle on the floor.

"So, the football player..." I told Dillon when I called him that night.

"Yes...?"

"He is so cute. He's teaching me how to cook!"

"So, he's a football player and a miracle worker?"

"That's what I'm saying. And a saint."

"Okay, now I'm pretty sure you're making this up. Because, let me tell you, I've dated some of the guys out there and none of them are like that. If they weren't all so hot, I would date women and never look back."

"Would you?" I asked doubtfully.

"Okay, fine. I would continue dating them and complain more."

"I don't know. Guys seem pretty great to me," I said, thinking about the way Cali looked at me.

"Says the virgin who met the perfect guy on his first attempt.

"I didn't say he was perfect."

"So, what? Perfect adjacent? That's still a pretty good neighborhood."

"He's a pretty great guy," I told my friend, falling for Cali a little more.

Waffles were a lot more complicated than I thought. There was something called a batter with a ton of ingredients and you needed a waffle maker. Luckily, Cali had one. On top of that, you had to know exactly when to turn the contraption off with nothing but the way it smelled.

What the hell? There was no way I was ever gonna get this. But they sure tasted good.

"Do you have any berries?" I asked, remembering the waffles I had had in Belgium.

"I don't think we do. But they're in season. I'm sure we can find them somewhere around here."

I paused.

"What do you mean?"

"If you are interested in berries, we can go pick some."

"Do you mean like a date?"

As soon as I said it, Cali's face turned red. Oh no. Had I just screwed everything up by suggesting that he go out on a date with me?

"Yeah, I guess. I mean, yeah. Like a date."

"Um, yeah. Of course. I mean, absolutely."

Cali smiled.

"Cool," he said casually.

"Yeah. Cool. When were you thinking?"

"I don't have any classes tomorrow. I'll probably spend a lot of the day at the hospital with my mother. But, maybe in the morning?"

I could barely contain myself I was so excited. My hands shook.

"Yeah, that sounds nice. Tomorrow morning."

"Cool!"

He got up.

"I should probably go. But I'll see you back here tonight."

"It sounds like a plan," I said, sounding like a dork.

"It's a plan," he said, briefly reaching out his hand to touch me but shifting away before he did. My chest clenched seeing the gesture.

Once he was gone, I made scrambled eggs and laid out the cereal and pastries for the guests. It was amazing that I did it considering how much blood I was losing to my erection. That and the fact that I was floating above my body.

For the rest of the day, all I could think about was my date with Cali. My skin tingled. To stop the ants from racing up and down my arms, I turned my attention to making the beds. I was determined to get it to look like what I saw on YouTube.

In the end, the beds never looked perfect, but I was getting better at it. And, more importantly, doing it took my mind off of things for a while.

Taking what I had learned from Cali, I then made myself lunch. How had I never made a sandwich before? Sure, it tasted pretty dry, but it totally qualified as edible.

After that, I went out for a walk. Heading back towards the diner, I entered the grocery store next to it. Because of my lessons with Cali, I saw everything in there in a new light. Sure, I still had no idea what most of the stuff was. But I was beginning to be able to imagine.

Continuing my walk, I began to think about my car. It was at the bottom of some mountain road. Was there anything in it that I needed? The only thing that came to mind was the cash I had in the trunk. There was still a few thousand dollars left. Staying at the bed-and-breakfast, it wasn't like I needed it. And, I always had my credit cards in case of emergency.

Knowing that it was probably too far to walk to in either case, I headed back when my tired legs replaced my endless excitement. Also, I knew that Cali could be arriving home soon. He didn't mention how many classes he had today or if he would be stopping by the hospital before returning to me, but I wanted to be there whenever he did.

He arrived a few hours later again looking exhausted. My heart broke for him.

"Would you like to go out to eat? My treat," I told him wanting to take care of him however I could.

"That's okay. I can cook something."

"You really don't have to.

"I know. I want to," he said, looking at me with a gaze that made my heart thump.

Hovering in the kitchen as he cooked, I felt like a lovesick puppy. It's a good thing that he didn't talk much because if he would have said anything, all I would have been able to do was giggle. Did every relationship feel like this? Was this what I had been missing? Or was what I felt when I was with Cali different?

Staring at him as we ate his delicious dinner, I decided that what we had was special. I then turned my thoughts to how I could get him to touch me. My hand would have been enough. Imagining his large fingers touching mine, I felt overwhelmed.

Looking at me between bites, he asked, "What are you thinking about?"

"What?" I said, feeling like I was caught red handed.

"Do you like it?" he asked, gesturing to the food.

I looked down, realizing I hadn't been eating.

"Yeah. Definitely," I said, returning to my meal

"So, how did you end up here?" he asked surprising me as the one making conversation.

"Do you mean in this town?"

"Yeah. There's a running joke here about how we're barely on the map. No one can figure out how people keep finding us."

"Oh. Luck, I guess. I was just driving. I didn't really have an itinerary when I left New York. But, when I started seeing landmarks that I had only heard about, I made a bit of a plan to visit as many of the famous national parks as I could find."

"There aren't any national parks around here," Cali said confused.

"No. But when I was searching online, a website said this town had more waterfalls than anywhere else in Tennessee. I figured it was worth seeing."

Cali offered a knowing smile and continued eating.

"What? Is that not true."

"No, it's true. It's just that the website was made by my brother."

"Do you mean Titus or Claude?"

He paused.

"Did I mention them to you?"

"No. I was talking to Marcus. He was saying that you just found out you had brothers you didn't know existed."

"I knew they existed. I just didn't know they were family."

"How did that happen?"

As soon as I said it, I knew I had hit a sore point. "It's okay if you don't want to talk about it."

"No, it's fine. I didn't know because my mama didn't tell me and Titus's mama never told him. I don't think Claude's mama knew."

"Wow! It must be weird knowing that this whole time your mother was keeping something from you."

The pain that he felt pulsed off of him. It took everything in me not to climb across the table and comfort him.

"Yeah. It's a point of contention. I hadn't visited Mama in a while because of it. Before the accident, I hadn't seen her in weeks. I would drive up from school and not stop by. What if I had lost her in that accident? Our argument would have been the last time she and I spoke," he said fighting back heartbreak.

This time I couldn't stop myself. Rushing to my feet, I circled the table and threw my arms around him. The back of his chair stopped my chest from connecting with his body. But I touched my temple to his feeling every bit of his pain.

"I'm so sorry about what happened to your mother. I'm so sorry," I told him, drowning in guilt.

He didn't respond. That was fine. He didn't need to tell me how upset he was with me. I'm just glad he allowed me to hold him. I couldn't change the hurt I had caused him. But I could do everything I could to make it up to him.

As I leaned over with our two bodies touching, the anguish I felt subsided just enough for me to breathe in his scent. It was a mixture of pine and a musk that drove me wild. Without realizing it, it got harder to breathe. I had to take deeper breaths, and when I did, I breathed in more of him.

I was quickly losing myself. When I couldn't take anymore, my fingertips tightened around his rippling muscles.

When he inhaled deeply, expanding his chest, I caught myself and let go. What was I doing? He was hurting, and I couldn't stop thinking about his naked body pressed against mine. He would hate me if he knew that I was the one responsible for him almost losing his mother. I had no right to be doing what I was.

Taking a moment to gather myself, I closed my eyes and took a deep breath. When I was again steady, I returned to my seat.

I was falling hard for Cali. I couldn't look at him. If I did, not only would he see what I had done, he would know how horrible of a person I was.

I thought I could escape my family's destiny. But I brought as much destruction as the rest of them did. I didn't deserve a guy like Cali.

Neither of us said a word until after both of our plates were clean. Even after that, we sat in silence unable to look at each other.

Not being able to take it anymore, I opened my mouth to speak. "I, ah…"

"We still picking berries in the morning?" He asked as if I would no longer want to.

Why would he think that?

"Of course. I've been thinking about it all day," I said, practically shivering from being overwhelmed with emotion.

"Good," he said flatly.

I wanted to climb into his brain and rip open all of his thoughts. I wanted to know everything about him.

I knew I didn't deserve something like that, though. I didn't deserve someone like him. These were moments stolen from a guy who deserved better.

If I were a good person at all, I would disappear in the middle of the night and never come back. But I was my father's son. Whether I liked it or not. We hurt others. And as much as I didn't want to, I was going to continue hurting this beautiful man.

"How can you tell when they're ripe?" I asked Cali, staring down at the prickly bush in front of me.

"The color, mostly," he said moving to my side. Sometimes you can squeeze them."

Plucking a purple berry from the plant in front of both of us, he stood pinching the fruit.

"There should be some give when you squeeze it. If it's hard, it's not ripe. See?" he said, rolling the berry into his palm.

Staring at his hand, my heart thumped. I was about to touch him. As I reached for the fruit, my fingertips lightly touched his rugged skin. I explored every ridge.

When the fruit was between my fingers, I rolled my hand, exploring his fingers with the back of mine. My touch begged for him to hold me. When his grip lightly tightened, I lost my breath. I yearned for more. But instead, I tested the berry as he watched.

"Yes, I see what you mean. It's soft but really sturdy. Dependable, I imagine," I said, staring into his eyes.

He didn't respond. Maybe I had taken it a step too far. But, wasn't this a date? Hadn't he said that? Didn't boys hold hands on dates? Or was that only what heterosexual couples did?

Maybe, he didn't actually think of this as a date. All he had suggested was for us to pick berries. Maybe I was looking too much into it.

"Have you ever been on a date with a guy before?" I asked him, desperately needing to know.

His fair skin turned a shade pinker. He was this large intimidating man yet he seemed so vulnerable. It was adorable. It made me want him more.

"I'm not great at this type of stuff," he admitted, averting his eyes.

"No, I didn't mean it like that. It's just that I haven't. I don't want to screw things up. I mean, if there's anything to screw up. I don't exactly have much experience with stuff like this."

"Like what?"

"Boys?"

"Girls?" Cali asked vulnerably.

I laughed.

"No, definitely not with that."

He averted his eyes before returning his gaze to mine.

"Are you gay?" he asked softly.

"Couldn't you tell? I thought everybody could."

Cali blushed.

"Are you?"

"I mean, I like girls too. At least, I have in the past. I might like boys more, though."

"When did you realize that?"

"Maybe when I realized that most of the people I jerk off to were boys," he said embarrassed.

"So, have you ever been with a guy?"

"I've done stuff. Mostly after a few drinks at parties. Nothing serious. What about you?"

"I've liked guys since I could remember. They've always made me feel nervous when I'm around them, you know? But my best friend is the only other gay guy I know. And, he's not really my type, so…"

"What's your type?"

My eyes poured down his body like a waterfall. I couldn't tell him what I was thinking. I didn't want to ruin things before they began. I opened my mouth hoping something else would come out. But before I could stop myself, I heard someone say the word, "You."

Staring up at him, all I could do was swallow. He was just staring at me. Why wasn't he saying anything?

I wanted to scream for him to say something. But instead, he slowly lifted his left hand and wrapped his large grip around my bicep. Turning me towards him, he moved inches from my body. I hadn't realized he was so tall.

What was he doing? I shook, not knowing what to expect. I felt so small and helpless being consumed by his body heat. And when he brushed the back of his hand against my hair, he gently touched the top of my earlobe. A chill washed through me.

I wanted him. I needed every part of him. So when he gently palmed the back of my head, I lifted my chin. This was it. I closed my eyes waiting for his lips. I could feel his heat wash across my face. He felt like he was a hair's width away. I waited. I begged. And then he pulled away not kissing me.

I opened my eyes in time to see him let go of me and walk away. I parted my lips, unable to catch my breath. What had just happened? Had I done something wrong? I wanted to scream to him and tell him I hadn't wanted him to stop. But his attention had turned.

With his head lowered, he wandered through the bushes. Just like that, we had returned to simply picking berries. I wanted to cry. Instead, I joined him in our task. Reaching down, I used what he had taught me. Plucking the ripe one, I placed them into my bowl.

Chapter 6

Cali

I should have kissed him, I kept repeating, torturing myself as I did.

"Are you here with us?" Titus asked, rescuing me from my spiraling thoughts.

"Yeah. What's up?" I said, returning to our conversation.

Titus was staring at me. And even though Claude was only present over FaceTime, I could feel his eyes as well.

"You worried about your mother?" Titus said from his desk chair at the far corner of the room.

My eyes bounced between my two brothers. They were worried about me. It felt nice having someone who was.

"Nah. I'm fine."

"You know you could tell us if there's something you need, right?" Claude said, getting Titus's confirmation.

"I appreciate that. That's not it, really."

"Then, what's up?" Titus asked, pressing me to tell him more than I knew.

What *was* up with me? Was it just that I had screw things up with Hil by not making a move? Was it the whole thing about being with a guy?

I was definitely interested in Hil. There was no doubt about that. I had never before felt anything like what I felt when I was with him. That wasn't it. It was that... Hell, I didn't know what it was.

"There's a guy," I blurted out before realizing it.

As soon as I said it, I burned with embarrassment. Sure, I had told Titus about my interest in guys. But there's a difference between having an interest and acting upon it. And, this was the first time I shared anything like this with Claude. Yeah, he liked Titus's boyfriend as much as I did. But that didn't mean he would feel the same when it came to me.

When neither of them responded, something inside me hurt.

"You know what, never mind," I said, regretting that I had brought it up.

"No. Don't mind us. We're both probably just a little surprised," Titus said.

"What are you talking about? I told you I liked guys."

"Yeah. But you're implying that you like someone, so I'm just trying to figure out what's wrong with him. Wait, does he already have a boyfriend? Because that would make a lot more sense," Titus said with a smirk.

"Fuck you," I said when I realized he was making fun of me.

Both guys laughed. It pissed me off, but only a little. Mostly, it just relaxed me. One of Titus's skills was knowing how to make people feel comfortable. It was one of the things I admired about him.

"Come on. You know I was just joking. Any guy would be crazy lucky to have you like them. Tell us about him. Is it someone from the team?" Titus asked confused.

It took me a moment to decide what I should tell them. I know my brothers were just busting my balls, but still.

"You know how my mother was in that accident?"

"Of course," Claude said from the other end of the phone.

"It was his car that my mother was driving. He staying at the bed-and-breakfast."

"Oh, fuck," Titus said with a curse word I rarely heard him use.

"Yeah. He's been staying there ever since. He's actually helping me take care of the place. It's the only way I can attend classes."

"So, if he's there," Claude began, "why are you in your dorm room now?"

"I don't know," I said lying.

"Because, it seems to me, if you like him, you should be spending time there instead of 100 miles away."

"We kind of had a date today."

"Wait, what?" Titus said shocked. "And this is the first time you're telling me about him?"

"What's more surprising is that you're surprised by that," Claude said, teasing Titus at my expense.

"You know what, never mind," I said wishing I had never brought this up.

"No. Come on. What's the use of having brothers if you can't tease them?" Claude said sincerely. "Seriously, you know you can talk to us about anything. You know that, right?"

I didn't respond. The truth was that I didn't know that. Trusting people didn't exactly come easily to me.

For a long time, I'd been living my life waiting for the other shoe to drop. The truth was that, although I'd never felt anything like I have for Hil, I have had strong feelings for a boy before. It was one of those things that sneaks up on you after spending a lot of time together.

Making friends had always been hard for me. When I was a kid, I was pretty shy. So, when this kid named Tim sat next to me at lunch and started talking to me like we had known each other forever, it meant a lot. We were both ten years old at the time, and he had been in my class a number of years. We had never been friends, though. But in that one conversation, everything changed.

It didn't take long for us to start sending almost every moment together. We would ride our bikes through the woods. We would go fishing together. Whenever we could, we would sleep over to each other's house. And it didn't take long before I started realizing that I liked him more than I should have.

He was the first person I fell in love with. It was because of him that I realized I liked guys as well. So, when he got sick and my mother explained that he wouldn't be getting better, it hurt. Eventually, he had to be taken to a hospital a few states over. And before I could convince my mother to take me to see him, he died.

I had never felt pain like that. It was like someone had reached into my chest and had ripped my heart out. It hurt too much to pretend that I would be all right. And when I read the note that he had left me knowing that his time was almost up, I became inconsolable.

From the grave he had admitted that he had loved me too. In fact, the reason he had started talking to me that first time was because he had had feelings for me from the moment he saw me in kindergarten. It had just taken him that long to gather the courage to say hello.

I couldn't go through that type of pain again. I had to shut down my ability to feel just to be able to get out of bed in the morning. Food lost its flavor.

Now, here Hil was making me feel things I had promised I never would. I was struggling. So, I wasn't in the mood to be teased about it by my brothers.

"You're not really upset with us, are you?" Titus asked, appearing like he felt bad.

"Nah, it's all good."

"Are you sure? You know we love you, right? We brothers have to stick together. No one is going to have our backs like we do. All three of us have been lied to our entire lives. They're still not telling us the truth. But we will always be there for each other. You know that, right?"

As much as I might not have been ready to feel that, I knew it.

"I know," I said, feeling better than I had.

Maybe I wasn't looking to talk about what happened between me and Hil. Maybe I just needed to hear that someone had my back. Titus and Claude did. I knew that. Whatever damage I had done between me and Hil, I would figure out. And if I needed them, my brothers would be there to help me.

"Do you know if Quin is hosting a game night anytime soon?" I said, changing the topic.

"Probably. You know Quin," Titus said.

Titus always assumed that I knew Quin better than I did. It was probably because he and his boyfriend both knew Quin so well. Titus's boyfriend Lou has been roommates with Quin for the past three years. And it was because Quin and his boyfriend had come to our town looking for Quin's boyfriend's birth parents that Titus decided to enroll in East Tennessee University.

The two of them went back a few years. I was younger than all of them. I was more like the roommate Titus allowed to tag along when the group hung out together.

"Could you find out?"

"Of course. What's up? Feeling like losing to Quin and Cage at a board game?"

Quin was a literal genius, and he and his boyfriend we're considered the power couple in our group. There was no beating Quin at any game that required strategy. And there was no beating the two of them when they teamed up together.

"It's just that Hil was telling me that he didn't have many friends growing up. So, I thought it would be good to introduce him to a few of mine. A game night would be the least intimidating way, I'm thinking."

Both Titus and Claude stared at me. The length of time it was taking for them to speak was making me uncomfortable.

"You got it, bro," Titus eventually said with a smile. "We got your back," he confirmed with a tight-lipped nod.

Chapter 7

Hil

"I told you. We got up early, went to his truck, drove to a spot in the woods, hiked for about a quarter of a mile, and then picked berries," I said to Dillon.

"And this whole time he didn't say anything weird?" he asked with the serious tone he got when we were trying to figure out a problem together.

"Something weird? I'm lucky if I can get him to say anything at all."

"And after that, he just dropped you back and took off. He didn't call you letting you know that he wasn't coming home or something?"

"No. He said he would be visiting his mother for the rest of the day. But I was expecting him to come back for dinner."

"Do you think something could have happened to him?"

"Dillon, that's all I can think about," I said, finally admitting what I wouldn't dare to say. "What if the person who ran my car off the road did the same to Cali? What if he's lying in a ditch somewhere? I don't know if I can handle that. What if I'm the reason two people I liked got hurt?"

"Hil, you can't think like that. You don't know why your friend's mother ended up driving off the side of the road. Whatever you say, you'll just be guessing. And I'm sure Cali is just off doing football things."

"Football things? Like what?"

"I don't know. Putting on jerseys with numbers on the back? Slapping other guys' butts?"

"You think he could be out slapping other guy's butts? Oh my God, it's worse than I thought."

There was a silence on the phone before Dillon eventually laughed.

"Okay, Hil, I'm going to assume that you realize you might be jumping the gun and worrying about nothing. Yes, it's a little weird that you haven't heard from him since your date. But it hasn't even been twenty-four hours. It's too soon to file a missing persons' report."

"You think I'm being ridiculous, don't you?"

Dillon again became quiet.

"I don't think you're being ridiculous. You're basing what could happen on your family's crazy life. But Cali isn't a part of your world. And you're in a small town in the middle of nowhere. I don't even know where you are. So, the fact that you are freaking out, although reasonable, isn't necessary considering the context."

"Wow! When did you get so smart?"

"I'm a college guy now. You should try it. And remind me again why you aren't here with me?"

"Do you seriously think my father would let me go to school without ten bodyguards surrounding me at all times? Could you imagine me going to a frat party? Everybody would love me."

"You do know that at some point you're going to have to stand up to your father, right?"

"It's easier said than done."

"This is something I've never understood, Hil. Is it that you're afraid of your father?"

"No. I know my father loves me. I know that he will do anything to protect me. It's just that no one says no to my father. Not even me. And I know he makes the decisions he does because he's looking out for me.

"You forget that you and I come from different worlds. The rules in my world are different. My father always says, 'Raising a lion like he's your pet cat will get it killed in the jungle'."

"So, what does that mean? That he can make every decision for you until you're trampled by elephants?"

"I'm on this trip because I'm trying to prove to him that I can make it on my own, remember? And maybe if he sees what I'm capable of, he'll free me."

"Or maybe he's just waiting for you to be a lion and just take your freedom," Dillon suggested.

I thought about that. Was that what my father wanted? Wasn't that what Remy did? My brother never let our father tell him what he could do. Not even when we were kids. Was my mistake that I always listened to what my father said? Would my father have respected me more if I hadn't?

"Hi!?" I heard Cali say before hearing a knock on my bedroom door.

"Dillon, I'll call you later. Cali's back."

"Okay. But don't give him a pass on not calling you. You deserve better than that."

"I'll call you later," I told him before ending the call and hurrying to the door.

Readying myself to see him, I didn't know how to feel. But the moment I stood in front of him, staring into those gorgeous, soulful eyes, I knew how I felt.

"I'm so happy to see you," I said, unable to stop myself.

Cali leaned back, surprised at my response.

"Yeah, me too," he said seeming disarmed.

"How's your mother? Did you spend the night at the hospital?"

"She's coming along. No, I went back to campus. My brothers and I have this thing we do on Saturdays."

"Really? That's awesome. What is it?"

"It's nothing special. It's just when we usually have time to hang out with each other. I probably should have told you that I wasn't gonna be back," he said lowering his eyes with guilt.

"No," I said relieved. "Why would you have to tell me? You don't owe me anything."

"But still, I could have called," he admitted.

"I'm just happy you're safe."

When I said that, he stared at me again. Realization washed through him.

"Right. Sorry. What are you doing tonight?"

My heart raced. Was he about to ask me on another date?

"I don't know. Do you have any suggestions?"

"My friends sometimes do game night on Sundays. I was wondering if you wanted to join me," he said more nervously than I would have guessed a man as big as him would be.

"Yeah, of course. I would love to meet your friends," I said beside myself.

"Great," he said relieved. "I think you'll like them. They're all really friendly. They're a great bunch of guys. You'll also meet their boyfriends."

"Wait, all of your friends are gay?"

"Mostly they're bisexual. Titus's boyfriend Lou is gay, I think. I don't know about Quin. But I think you'll like them. You should fit right in," he said with kindness in his eyes.

I barely knew what to say. I had never been a part of a group before. The fact that he was doing this for me almost brought me to tears. It took everything in me to hold them back.

"Thank you. I'm sure your friends are great. I mean, they're friends with you, aren't they?" I said with a smile.

Cali smirked.

"You should be ready to head out around five. We'll probably order a few pizzas there," he told me as he shifted to walk away.

"What are you up to today?" I asked hoping he would want to spend it with me.

"Oh, I have an errand I need to run. I'll be back. You just be ready for five," he said before disappearing into his mother's room.

Listening to him leave, I decided to take my mind off our exciting night by cleaning up the place. I rearranged and fluffed the cushions. I swept downstairs. And I made my first ever attempt at cleaning a bathroom.

I don't know how I felt about the last one. I still liked knowing that I was the one keeping the business afloat. But bathrooms aren't fun to clean. Who knew?

When Cali returned, I was sitting on the back deck admiring the view. The bed-and-breakfast overlooked a valley layered in pine trees with a mountainous backdrop covered in the midst of a waterfall. Growing up in New York I didn't know that places like this existed.

"What are you doing out here?" Cali asked joining me.

"Enjoying the view. I can't imagine growing up every day looking at this."

"I can't imagine growing up in a city."

"It's nothing like this. We have a view, and it's nice, but it's of the New York skyline."

"That does sound nice."

"But it's all concrete. In the distance, you can see the river, but looking out to this," I said pointing to the landscape in front of us, "it makes you feel alive."

Cali looked at the view as if seeing it for the first time. He took a moment to admire it and then turned back to me.

"Are you ready to go?"

"I've been ready since the moment you told me," I said with a smile.

"Then I have a surprise for you," he said with more excitement than I had ever seen on him.

"What's that?"

"Let's head out," he said leading me through the house and onto the front porch. There was a truck parked on the driveway that I hadn't seen before. "How about you drive?"

"You want me to drive?"

"Yeah. It's your truck. You may as well get used to driving it," he said, cracking a smile.

"My truck?"

"It's not much but I figure it's better than being stuck here all day. It's yours for as long as you need it."

"You're giving me your truck?"

"It's not mine. It belongs to a friend. But he doesn't need it, and since you lost your car in the accident, we both thought you should have it."

Stunned, I stared at the truck and then turned to Cali. I barely knew what to say.

"I know it's not much to look at…"

"No, it's beautiful. No one's ever done something so nice for me before."

"You only say that because you haven't driven it," Cali said with a chuckle. "Believe me, it's not that big a deal. But I want you to be able to get around if you need to. It's the least I can do."

I wanted to kiss Cali so badly that my heart hurt. He had to be the sweetest, kindest guy I had ever met. I stared at him not knowing what to do with myself. I was torn between collapsing into tears and throwing my legs around his waist and losing my tongue down his throat.

"We should head out. We can take the long way to give you a little practice driving a clunker like this."

Getting into the truck, I had a feeling I never got driving in any of my family's fancy cars. There was something about this ten-year-old pickup; it felt like love. There's a difference when you get a gift from someone who has everything compared to getting one from someone who has so little.

Cali's gesture made me feel special. Like I was valued. Nothing my father had ever given me made me feel like that.

Pulling away, the rumble of the engine gave me a thrill. Gripping the oversized wheel, I felt like I was reigning in a monster. It definitely took some getting used to. But by the time we pulled up to his friend's two-story ranch house, I was feeling confident.

"What are your friends' names again?" I said staring at the place nervously.

"It's Quin and Cage who live here. Quin goes to school with me and Cage graduated two years ago. Now he teaches football at our local high school.

"Titus will also be there with his boyfriend Lou. Claude will be there, and I think Kendall will be there as well. Kendall is the boyfriend of Cage's brother. Cage's brother plays professional football. I'm not sure why he's not in town right now, but Kendall is a part of the group so he's here."

"Marcus isn't going to be here?"

"Marcus?"

"Yeah, he's the only other person I know."

"He's not really friends with Quin or Cage, and they're the ones who usually host."

"Do you not like Marcus, or something?

Cali looked at me confused.

"No, he's fine. Why do you ask?"

"He thinks you don't like him."

Cali turned away without responding.

"We should head in," he said, exiting the truck.

My heart thumped as we approached the front door. This new experience was at once terrifying and exhilarating.

The person opening the door had curly hair and a broad smile.

"Cali, you made it. And this must be Hil?" he said, turning to me.

"Hil, this is Titus," he said, introducing us.

"The brother," I said, seeing the resemblance.

I struck out my hand for a handshake when Titus stepped forward brushing it aside.

"We don't shake hands here, we hug," he said, throwing his arms around me.

I was surprised, but I loved it. After Titus, I met Quin, Lou, and Kendall, who were small guys like me. And then Cage and Claude who were both muscular and gorgeous.

Did you say your name was Claude?" I asked, trying not to seem too surprised.

Claude looked at Titus and Cali. They all laughed.

"Yes, I'm the black sheep of the family," he said referencing his brown skin.

Out of all of them, Claude was the most regal. In a room full of jocks, Cage was probably the most like a quarterback. Quin seemed like the most popular. Lou seemed to be the most fun-loving. Kendall seemed the most reserved. And Titus seemed the most like a great guy. I wasn't sure how Cali fit into the group. But he seemed as comfortable here as I felt welcomed.

Once the games began and the drinks started flowing, I learned a lot about everyone. I wasn't the only one from New York. Quin was as well. He grew up in a building overlooking Central Park. Not only did his family have money, but they we're worth billions. It was amazing that he was so down to earth.

"Do you miss the city?" I asked him, fascinated by his story.

"Not really. Everything I need I can find here," he said humbly.

"He likes hanging amongst the common folk," Titus joked.

Quin didn't respond.

"Don't say it like that," Lou added.

"Then, how am I supposed to say it?"

"You know exactly how," Lou insisted. "You say that he's slumming it with the common folk. And we mere mortals are grateful to be around one of the gods."

Everybody laughed.

Titus leaned towards me.

"We just like to tease Quin because he's so great at everything. It makes us feel better for when he kicks our ass later on. The guy is a literal genius. Quin, say something genius," Titus said, turning everyone's attention to Quin.

"Titus, you're a moron," he said flatly.

"Come on, baby," Cage replied. "It doesn't take a genius to figure that out."

Everyone laughed.

"You got me," Titus said leaning back.

"But he's my moron," Lou said, throwing his arms around Titus and giving him a kiss.

"Is it always like this?" I whispered to Cali.

"Mostly. But they are in rare form tonight."

"I like it," I said, slowly realizing what I had been missing. "Thank you for bringing me," I said, squeezing his hand. Cali replied with a tight-lipped smile and a nod.

After a game called Wavelength, we decided to play Scrabble in teams. With Claude partnering with Kendall, it started out as a match of couples. But when Quin and Cage pulled into a lead that we had no chance of catching, the other three teams worked together to give the rest of us a chance. Quin still wiped the floor with us.

"Do you see what I mean?" Titus asked in affable defeat.

It was a fun night. Eventually when it ended, I drove us back to the bed-and-breakfast and Cali walked me to my door.

"Thank you for one of the best nights of my life," I said, standing in the doorway inches from him.

"I'm glad you had fun. They are great friends to have. If you stick around, you can call them up at any time."

"If I stick around?"

"Yeah. You know, if you want to."

"Do you want me to?"

Cali didn't answer, but the look on his face sent and tingle down to my sex. I could feel his body heat envelop me. It was intoxicating.

Standing as close to him as I was, I could barely control myself. He had to be the most gorgeous guy I'd ever met in my life. So when he pushed his thick fingers through my hair, grabbed the back of my head, and pulled my lips to his, my knees wobbled.

I hadn't imagined a kiss could feel like this. I was lightheaded. I was more aroused than I had ever been in my life. Not wanting it to end, I wrapped my arms around him exploring the rippling muscles on his back. He was a god, and I worshipped him. So when he released me and I returned to earth, I was awestruck and hurting for more.

"Goodnight," he said as the back of his hand traveled down my neck and chest. I was hoping it would reach my cock. It didn't. Mourning the loss of his touch, I ached.

"Goodnight," I said, eventually forcing it out.

Watching him walk to his room, I prayed he wouldn't go. He looked back. I could read his thoughts. He was considering joining me in my room.

I wanted so badly for him to do it. But, painfully, he didn't. Gently closing the door behind him after entering his room, he was gone. I burned for him.

Chapter 8

Cali

As I sat waiting for my mother's doctor, I couldn't stop thinking about our kiss. To feel Hil in my arms was like waking up from a bad dream. The endless waves of pain that I felt after losing Tim had calmed. For the first time in years, the storm clouds had lifted. I could see in vivid color and Hil was a ball of light.

I needed to be near him. I wanted to spend every second holding his hand. And when darkness fell, I wanted to strip him naked and to make him mine.

Feeling my cock grow hard thinking about it, I burned for his body. I wanted to hold his small wrists in my hands, pin them over his head, slide my knees under his legs, and push my cock into him. I was drunk just thinking about it.

I also wanted to do everything I could to make him happy. He was everything I ever wanted in a guy. And I was ready to make his happiness my purpose in life.

"Cali?" My mother's snowy topped, dark-skinned doctor said, grabbing my attention.

"Dr. Tom?" I said, standing up and immediately realizing that I shouldn't have.

"I have some good news and I have some news that isn't quite as good," he began in a solemn tone. "The good news is that there is no need for her to remain in the hospital. There's nothing that we could do here that couldn't also be done for her at home."

Relief washed through me.

"That's great. What's the other news?"

"She's going to need surgery if she's going to walk again."

The skin on my face prickled hearing his words. I was stunned. The one thing that had always been true about my mother was that she had boundless energy. Growing up, I always found it tiring. She would keep going and going while all I wanted to do was lock myself in my room and pretend nothing existed.

Running from project to project was a part of who my mother was. The thought of her not being able to walk again was like losing her to someone I wouldn't recognize.

"You don't have to worry. It's a simple procedure. I've done it many times. However, I'm told you don't have insurance."

"No, we don't. But we can pay for it cash, right?"

"Of course. And the hospital will certainly adjust the costs taking your situation into consideration. But, it's still not a small sum."

"Don't worry, I'll get it. You can do whatever you need to do to prepare for the surgery. I promise."

"You have some time. Your mother still needs more time to recover. Maybe in a few weeks?"

"That won't be an issue. Just tell me what you need, when you need it, and I'll make sure you have it," I told him, knowing that we didn't have that type of money in our bank account.

I had seen my mother's hospital bill so far. That alone would bankrupt us. Her surgery would put us in a hole that would take a lifetime to dig our way out of. But I would do whatever I had to do to take care of her like she had done for me. I would do anything for my mother.

Leaving the doctor, I joined my mother at her bedside. As she looked up at me, I noticed the pink returning to her cheeks. The black and blue marks that had consumed her body were receding. She really was looking better, but shifting my gaze to her legs, I was filled with heartbreak.

"What did the doctors tell you?" she asked, unable to mask her Jamaican accent like she usually did.

"He said that you can come home," I said, forcing a smile.

"Did he tell you about the walking thing?" she said, cutting right to the point as usual.

I shook my head.

"Don't worry about it. I have friends I can call up."

"I'll take care of it. You just focus on getting better. The doctor says you still have some recovering to do before he can schedule anything. You worry about that. I'll take care of the rest."

My mother smiled, trusting that I would. She then gave me her classic wry smile.

"You know he was exaggerating, right?"

"What do you mean?"

"I can walk. It's just slower. It will give other people time to catch up."

"You better start thinking about rehab or whatever they have lined up for you and stop thinking about who would win in a race."

"There are things I need to do. We have guests scheduled to come in. Rooms need to be prepared. There is this little thing called a broom. I know you've never heard of it. But it needs to be swept across the floor at least once a week," she said, teasing me.

"Don't worry, Mama, it's being taken care of. All you need to do is focus on getting better."

"I told you, Cali, your job is to go to class and focus on school. That's where your future is. You can't let anything distract you."

"I've been going to classes. I haven't skipped a one."

She looked at me confused.

"You remember Hil?"

Anguish washed across her face. "Do you mean the boy whose car I destroyed?"

"It wasn't your fault, Mama. He knows that someone ran you off the road. He's not upset about it. And he's been staying at our place since the accident."

"Shit, I just remembered, I scheduled someone in his room."

"We know. He has been staying in my room."

"Your room?"

"Yeah. I hope you don't mind but I've been staying in yours."

"Oh," she said with a bigger smile. "I guess we're going to get pretty cozy in there when I get back."

I stared at her blankly. I hadn't thought about that. With my mother coming home, she would probably need her space to recuperate. Where would I sleep? All of the rooms were full, and there is no way I was going to let Hil sleep on a couch or move out.

I continued to think about this as I drove home. I felt like there were things I needed to do to prepare for her return. I wasn't sure what they were at this point. But the thought of them felt overwhelming.

Pulling up to the house, I stared at the truck parked outside. It had taken some effort to get it for Hil, but the feeling I had giving it to him made me want to wrap my arms around him and never let him go. Yes, he was owed it, considering that he would still have his own car if Mama hadn't been driving it. But also, it was my way of telling Hil how much I wanted him to stick around.

I was starting to need him. It was crazy. We had just met. But our kiss told me everything I needed to know.

He was the most incredible guy I had met in my life. His enthusiasm was infectious. I might have sat in my truck and thought about all of the ways I was going to be unable to live without him when he stepped onto the porch and met my eyes with a smile.

Getting out, I strolled up to him. God, I wanted to kiss him again. And the way he looked at me made me believe that he wanted it to. This wasn't the time, though. There were more important things than we had to do. Mama was coming home. We had to get things ready.

"How is she?" Hil asked with genuine concern.

"Dr. Tom said she can come home."

His face sparkled with joy.

"That's amazing!"

I lowered my head, remembering the rest of what the doctor had said.

"What's the matter?"

I pulled myself together. "Nothing. You're right, it's amazing."

Hil didn't quite believe me, but he didn't push the issue. Instead, he recaptured his brilliant smile and wrapped his arm around mine.

"Then I guess we need to prepare."

"Yeah," I agreed, knowing there was an elephant in the room that we needed to talk about.

Together, we came up with a plan.

"I don't know how you feel about this, but if she can't get around, I can help her. And, you know, things like getting to the bathroom, helping her in the shower... the things a son would never want to do with their mother," he offered, further chipping at the wall guarding my heart.

"I can't ask you to do that."

"You didn't ask. I'm offering. It would be my privilege to be able to do this for... her," he said looking into my eyes.

I ached loving him so much. I had no idea how I was going to get through this. Yet, every step of the way, he had me.

I..." I began not being able to say more.

"You, what?" he asked gently.

How was I supposed to explain to him how much he had done for me? It was everything. I'd spent my whole life holding myself back, sure that if I let myself need anybody, they would leave me. But somehow, here he was holding my hand. The conflict in me made me want to scream to the heavens. I didn't.

"Nothing. Thank you," I said, saying it the best way I could.

"No, thank you," he said with a tear in his eye.

"Why are you thanking me?"

"Because you've given me something I've wanted all of my life."

"What's that?"

"A reason to live," he said with tears streaming down his cheek.

My heart broke hearing his words. The idea that someone like him would say something like that, it destroyed me. Using my thumb to wipe his trail of tears, I cradled his head, allowing my thumb to caress the top of his ear. He leaned into my touch.

Eventually pulling ourselves together, we sat and made a list of all of the things we needed to do. Hil mentioned things like getting a non-slip mat for the tub and handles she could use to get in and out. They weren't things I could buy in town. So, between classes and my trips back to Snow Tip Falls, I slowly acquired everything from the list.

By the third day when Mama was scheduled to come home, there was only one thing we hadn't yet talked about. It felt like we were both dancing around the topic. He knew he wasn't going anywhere, and I knew there wasn't anywhere else I could sleep.

"So, do you think your mother would be okay with me doing a little couch surfing?"

"What do you mean?"

"That's what they call it, right?" he asked vulnerably.

"I'm sure she'll be okay with it, but you're not the one staying on the couch. I am."

"No, you're not. You have a bedroom. I can't kick you out of it. If it's necessary, I can find somewhere else to stay. But, I'd love to stick around town if you'll have me," he asked with a crinkle in his forehead.

"Don't be silly. You're not going anywhere. If anything, I'll find somewhere else to sleep. I could stay with Titus or Claude. I'm sure neither of their mothers would mind. They've already offered anything they could do to help."

"But, what if your mother needs you in the middle of the night for something I can't help her with? You need to be here."

"Well, you're not going anywhere. I won't let you."

"What are we gonna do?" he asked, looking up into my eyes longingly.

I opened my mouth to speak but couldn't.

"What?" he asked desperately.

"Nothing."

He closed the distance between us and took my hand, lifting my gaze from the floor to meet his.

"No, say it."

Staring at him I never felt more naked in my life. My heart thumped thinking about what I wanted. Did he want me to? Maybe I shouldn't say it.

"I mean, if you trust me…"

"I trust you!" he blurted out, encouraging me to speak.

"Then maybe neither of us have to go anywhere," I said hesitantly.

"Uh-huh," he said, encouraging me to go on.

"I mean, my bed's pretty big. We could both fit in it if we want."

"We want… I mean, don't we? Don't we both want?" he asked, begging me to say yes.

"There's nothing I would want more," I told him, meaning every word.

His demeanor brightened.

"Then it's settled. We'll both stay in your room," he said, as if it were the most obvious thing in the world.

Driving my mother home from the hospital, my hands were shaking. My mother's care was now up to me. I had consulted with her doctors and I had Hil's help, but it ultimately came down to me. I was going to do anything I had to do to help her recover, but she made me promise that it wouldn't come at the expense of school. It was an impossible bargain, but I had to keep it.

On top of that, there was Hil. How would my mother respond to what was developing between us. I hadn't told her how I felt about guys.

Yeah, there have been times when my fair skin might have given away my feelings. But there was no way for her to know how I truly felt. I never told her.

So, from knowing nothing, she was going to see Hil and me sharing a bed. How would I explain that? And as sure as I was about my feelings for him, I still didn't know how public I wanted it to be.

It had been great bringing him to game night. He fit in better than I ever have. Quin had treated him like the brother he never had. In one night, Hil had made himself a part of the group—a feat that I still wasn't sure I had accomplished.

But, winning the guys over was easy. There was also the rest of the town and even my teammates back At East Tennessee. It wasn't that I didn't think they would accept him or us. It was that being with him revealed a part of myself to the world that I wasn't ready to face.

It was more than that he was a guy. Being with Hil meant that I needed others. And, I get it, everybody needs somebody. But I wasn't sure I was ready for everyone to know that that included me.

Arriving home, Hil immediately came out to greet us.

"Cali told me how much you've been helping with the business. I can't thank you enough," Mama said, staring at him through the open truck door.

"Of course," he said heartfully. "Anything you need, just let me know. It's not a problem at all," he replied with his hand on his heart.

"He also told me that he's been teaching you how to cook," Mama said as we helped her into the house.

"It's more like he's been holding the fire extinguisher as I burn things," he joked.

"That's not what I hear. I was told you're cooking up a storm. You've been making breakfast for our guests?" she asked, having ascended the stairs to the porch.

"If you call putting out the cereal and Marcus's pastries making breakfast, then yeah," he said with a smile.

"You know that's not true. Hil has been scrambling eggs and making pancakes. He's even made waffles that rivals yours, Mama," I said, not allowing Hil to get away with putting himself down.

"Waffles that rival mine, huh?" she asked, revealing a hint of her competitive side.

Hil could not have been more embarrassed.

"Oh, no. They are edible at best. The ones Cali makes are out of this world. I just cover mine with enough fresh berries that you can't taste them."

"He doesn't know what he's saying, Mama. He'll have to cook some for you and you can tell him how good they are. It doesn't look like he's going to believe me."

"How can I? All you say are nice things."

"I say those nice things because you deserve it. If everyone was like you, this world would be a whole lot better place. I don't know what I would have done without you. I can't imagine what it might feel like to see you leave," I said, no longer having to come out to my mother.

Hil didn't respond with anything but a heartfelt smile. I was hoping I hadn't embarrass him. But he was an amazing guy. I couldn't just stand by and let him say those things about himself. My mother needed to know how wonderful he was. And if he wasn't going to speak up for himself, I was going to yell it from the rooftops.

After talking up his cooking abilities, he begged for me to be the one to cook dinner.

"I'll make breakfast," he said, psyching himself up.

"Anything you make will be amazing," I told him, knowing it was true.

After dinner and then helping my mother to her room, Hil and I stared at her not sure what to do next. "So, did you two figure out the sleeping arrangements?" my mother asked, embarrassing the hell out of me.

"Yeah. Since all of the rooms are booked, we decided I would just camp out on the floor of my room." "Are you sure about that? Your bed's pretty big. The two of you could probably fit in it, don't you think, Hil?" my mother asked with a big smile.

Hil blushed and then looked at me.

"Yeah, I guess. The bed is pretty big."

I did not like what Mama was doing.

"Anyway Mama, you have the bell right there in case you need help getting to the bathroom or anything. Don't be afraid to ring it. One of us will be right in.

"I'll try not to ring it at any inopportune moments," my mother said, having too much fun with her innuendos. "Goodnight, Mama," I said, clutching Hil's shoulder to guide him out.

"Yes, goodnight. And don't be afraid to ring that bell," Hil said before we both exited.

Behind her closed door, Hil looked at me.

"So, that was interesting," he said, unsure what to make of it.

"Yeah, imagine stuff like that your whole life."

"I don't know, I thought it was sweet. I could never imagine either of my parents doing something like that." he paused. "I mean, if she knows that, you know, you're into guys. You are into guys, aren't you?" he asked, biting his lip nervously.

"I'm at least into one guy," I admitted, looking at him.

"That lucky son of a bitch. Who is it? I'll kill him where he stands," he joked.

I laughed and then we both entered my bedroom and stared at the bed. As soon as I did, lust flashed through me. It was uncontrollable. Knowing what was about to happen, my cock got hard. I froze.

"What's the matter?" Hil asked when I didn't enter.

"Hil, are you sure you wanna do this?" I asked, unsure how much I would be able to resist.

Hil became serious. His quiet confidence was gone. Nervously, he stepped in front of me.

"I'm okay with it if you are." He looked away and shook his head as if attempting to find a different answer. "I mean, yes. I want to do this."

Reaching down, he took my hand. His warm flesh against mine sent a tingle that rippled through me. I wanted him. I'd never been more turned on in my life. But I also wanted to respect him. I didn't want to do anything that he wasn't ready for.

Because of that, I reeled in my desire. It nearly broke me, but I did. Still holding his hand, we entered the room. It was weird seeing Hil's stuff scattered around my familiar space. I liked it. I couldn't have guessed how much.

"Do you have to head back to campus in the morning?" Hil asked as he hovered around his travel bag.

"Yeah. But I'll be back early to help Mama settle in."

"I'll make waffles."

"I would like that. I think Mama would enjoy that too," I said, starting to relax. "We should probably head to bed. I'm thinking it's going to be a long day tomorrow."

"Of course," he said nervously.

Seeing how nervous he was, only made me want him more. I wanted to hold and take care of him. I wanted to protect him. And whether or not I admitted it, I wanted to slowly push my hard cock into him, listening to his light moans as I did.

I turned away when my cock began to throb. I didn't know how I was going to do this. It was taking everything in me not to race across the room, scoop him into my arms, and throw him onto the bed.

"What's the matter?" he asked, lightly wrapping his fingers around my bicep from behind.

I could feel his body heat. My heart thumped needing him. Did he know what he was doing to me? He couldn't consider what it might unleash.

I didn't speak. Instead, I pulled off my shirt. He let go of my arm as I did and then stepped back. I could still feel him there. And now I could feel his hot breaths on the skin of my back.

"Would you mind if I get comfortable?" he asked, sounding like he couldn't catch his breath.

"Sleep how you like," I said, still not looking at him.

Hearing his clothes rustle, I didn't turn around again until I heard him slip under the sheets. Hard as a rock, I still couldn't turn around. Even with my jeans on, there was no hiding it.

Knowing I was going to have to, I gathered my courage. As I did, Hil spoke.

"You can get comfortable too if you want. I've found that the room can get pretty hot at night."

Glancing at him without turning, something caught my eye. He had put his clothes on the foot of the bed. It was his shirt and underwear. Was he trying to tell me he was naked?

Burning desire ignited me. There was only so much I could do to stop myself. Turning around, I stared down at him. He looked so beautiful tucked beneath my sheets. He gazed back at me. I allowed him to get an eyeful before crossing the room and reaching for the light switch.

"You can turn on the night stand light," I said looking back at him.

With it on, I turned off the overhead light and circled the bed to the far side. Unbuttoning my jeans, I sat down. Pulling them off, I took a breath.

I could feel his eyes on me. It drew me to him with a power I couldn't defeat. Thinking I was going to keep my underwear on, in the last second, I pulled them off. Slipping under the sheets, I struggled to breathe. I was going insane fighting the urge to devour him. It took every ounce of my focus not to immediately pull him into my arms.

"Would you like me to turn off the light?" Hil asked nervously.

"Yeah," I told him and then closed my eyes, waiting for the click.

Surrounded in darkness, the room was silent. I could hear him breathe. It was interrupted and strained.

I was sure that if I wrapped my arms around him, it would help. Knowing that, there was little I could do to resist. I needed to protect him like I needed air. I was suffocating not being able to rescue him. I needed to at least touch him. So, slowly sliding my hand to him, my fingertips connected with his hip. His muscle tensed.

Waiting for a response, nothing came. Did he want me to touch him? Would he allow me to touch him more? I had to find out.

Slowly moving my fingertips onto the ridge of his pelvic bone, I palmed his flesh. I could confirm that he was naked. And he wasn't resisting. But I wasn't sure what I should do next.

Laying there, my fingers became restless. Not moving my thumb, I massaged his groin. With each grip, they got closer to his cock. I knew that I would only be able to go so far without hearing his voice. So, stopping tantalizingly close to his dick, I stilled my movements and waited.

I could feel his body twitch underneath me but I wasn't going to budge until I knew he wanted it. In my head I screamed for him to say it. Every second was torture.

When he finally moved, it wasn't how I expected. Rolling away from me onto his side of the bed, he lay there for only a moment before quickly inching back. With my hand transferred to his ass cheek, I felt every movement. When he was a breath away, I rolled onto my side allowing our steaming flesh to touch.

Wrapping my arm around him, I placed my hand on his chest. I could feel his heart. It was pounding.

Quickly he held my hand. I hadn't thought I could be aroused more, but I was. My cock flinched uncontrollably pushing against his crack. As it did, he tensed.

With every muscle in his body taught, he subtly rocked his hips against me. His cheeks were stroking my cock. Tilting my pelvis, I joined him. With each push, I slipped further between his mounds. And when I pulled back and gently gave him a thrust, he inhaled and gripped my hand telling me he wanted more.

Feeling that, I could no longer resist. Pressing my cock harder, I pulled my hand off of his chest and moved it to the side of his thigh. His hand followed mine, gripping tighter with everything that he liked.

When he felt the poke of my head, he dug in his fingertips. When I moved it to tickle the muscles of his opening, he gripped me so hard I thought something would break.

With the tip of my cock sitting on his opening, I pushed. It wasn't enough to enter him, but he squeaked. Testing again, he gave the same response. Needing more, I pushed harder. His puckered muscles continued to resist.

As much as I wanted him, I could have settled for just this. My head would have tested his opening all night if it wasn't for when his smooth body relaxed and his tempered voice squeaked, "Please."

That was all I needed to hear. Shifting away from him for only a second, I rolled to the far side of the bed and reached under it. Pulling out a condom and lube, I slipped one on and slathered my fingers with the other.

Again, touching his hole, but this time with my fingers, I pushed on it until I entered with a pop. Loosening him, his hips danced to my rhythm. After I pushed in a second finger and gently pried him open, I removed them, lubed my sheathed manhood, and rolled back into place.

As thick as I was, I knew my two fingers would have barely prepared him. I needed to take it slow. Pressing the head of my cock onto his opening, he reached back and grabbed my thigh. This was it. I wasn't going to stop. He twitched and moaned beneath me. But with a firm grip on his waist, I kept pushing and pushing until his muscles gathered around the rim of my cap and his tension released.

I was in him. I was in Hil.

Pausing for only a moment, I soon continued, slowly pushing the rest of me in him. It took a while. But when he again relaxed, I pulled out. When I pushed in again, it was quicker. With every thrust, Hil let go. And when all that was left was his moans of pleasure, I let go of his waist and reached for his cock.

He was as hard as I was. When I wrapped my fingers around him, his dick flinched. Fucking him and stroking his cock, my resistance was a dam under pressure.

Quickly crumbling, my thoughts spun. I was forgetting what I was doing. Soon, all that was left of me was my pleasure. And when my dam broke and I exploded into Hil, he came too.

Gripping me, Hil twitched violently. With my cock inside of him, I felt every one. When his calm was followed by involuntarily flinches, my dick flinched too. We continued like this until both of our exhausted bodies relaxed. And when my thick cock retreated, I gently slipped out of his ass.

Holding him for a second, I eventually rolled away and collected a towel. Handing it to him, he made quick work of it. Using it to clean myself off, I counted down the seconds until I could hold him.

I could never have imagined I could feel the way I felt with Hil's body pressed against mine. Gripping him tightly as we fell asleep, I knew I was in trouble. I now needed him to breath. I could no longer live without him.

Chapter 9

Hil

Waking up in Cali's arms, I didn't have to open my eyes to remember what had happened. I had lost my virginity to the greatest guy I could imagine. Feeling his naked body wrapped around mine, I never wanted him to let me go. I didn't know what I was missing all these years. I knew there was no way I would be able to go back.

I was happy. After a lifetime of worrying what my father thought and what my brother would say about me, I was free. Here, enveloped in the body heat of the greatest guy in the world, I felt accepted and whole.

I would have stayed in his arms until we both starved to death, and I wouldn't have regretted it for a second. But when I heard the bell we had given to Cali's mother, I knew our first great night together was at an end.

Waiting to see if Cali moved, I opened my eyes. His rough, large hands lay in front of me. Slipping my fingers between his, I felt tiny. I couldn't believe I was about to do this, but I was going to have to let him go.

If he wasn't going to see what his mother needed, I had to. I had promised to help him take care of her, and I didn't want to miss the opportunity. Feeling needed was new to me, and I liked it a lot.

Enjoying the last of his warm embrace, I squeezed his hand for a final time and gently removed his arm from around me. As soon as I did, he tightened his grip. God, did I love the way that felt. But I had to go.

When I lifted his arm again, he stirred.

"Where you going?" he said like a dog losing his bone.

"Your mother rang her bell. She might need to go to the bathroom or something," I explained.

It took him a moment to register my words. When he did, he sprung up.

"No. I've got it. You can rest. I'll be helping her a lot when you're gone. We may as well break the seal on it now."

Pulling out of his arms and looking back at him, I felt a rush reminding me of what I liked about him. His soulful eyes were hypnotic. Behind them, I could see a whole world. I wanted so much to be invited in. Until then, I would admire from afar.

Slipping out of bed and remembering I was naked, I stood with my back to Cali looking for my clothes. I could feel his eyes on me. Their warm caress reinvigorated my morning wood. Not as courageous as the night before, I hid my erection as I collected my underwear. Looking back as I pulled them on, I saw Cali's devilish smirk.

"What are you smiling about?" I asked him wanting to hear him say it.

"Have I told you how much I love your body?" he said to my surprise.

"No, I don't think you have."

"God, I love your body," Cali said, making it official.

"Yours isn't too bad either," I said, slipping on my jeans and then my shirt. "Maybe if you're still there when I get back, you can give me a better look at it. I don't think I saw enough last night," I said regretting my choice to leave.

What I had told him had been true. I barely saw anything of him last night. I certainly felt him. I was still feeling him. Maybe it was because I was a virgin, but Cali had felt huge. I wasn't a small guy, and he had to be twice my length and girth. Cali's cock was both overwhelming and addictive. I had never felt more complete than when he was inside of me.

Leaving our room and crossing the hall to his mother's, I talked my erection down and saw to Dr. Sonya's needs.

"I'm sorry I had to disturb you two, whatever you might have been doing," she said embarrassed.

"Don't even think about. We're both here to help you with whatever you need. You just let us know, and we'll be there," I told her sincerely.

What Dr. Sonya needed was help starting her day. First, she needed help getting to the bathroom. Then, she needed help changing, brushing her teeth, fixing her hair, and then getting back into bed. Thinking about Cali the entire time, I told Dr. Sonya that I was going to make breakfast and then hurried to our room.

Opening the door, I found the bed empty. Looking at the clock on the night stand, I saw it was later than I had thought. If Cali didn't leave soon, he would be late for class. So, instead of stripping down and waiting for him to return from the hallway bathroom, I headed downstairs to make him waffles and to begin our first day as whatever we were to each other.

Mixing the ingredients as I had been shown, it wasn't too long until I had a batter that dripped off the fork in clumps. It was the right consistency and as long as I didn't miss spots on the waffle maker with the nonstick spray, I had a good shot at not screwing it up.

When the first one came out golden brown, I was beside myself. Not only did they look good but they smelled fantastic. I couldn't take any credit for this. All I had done was not screw it up. This was Cali's family recipe. I was just grateful that he had shared it with me.

"I know what these waffles could use," I said aloud, "fresh berries," I said before pouring more batter into the waffle maker and hurrying to the door.

Slipping on shoes, I exited onto the porch. Although where Cali had taken me to pick berries was beautiful, I later learned that there were also wild bushes on the edge of their property where it met the woods.

Knowing there were a few ripe ones left from the last time I went picking, I headed to them. Not paying attention to the road in front of the property, I looked up when I heard a car engine startup and pull off.

The car I spotted looked as out of place in this small town as mine had. I had only caught the back of it, but I had seen enough luxury cars to know what it was. It had been a C-Class. It stood out like a sore thumb in the land of trucks.

Frozen, I considered what I had seen. Why was that car parked in front of the bed-and-breakfast? And why did it pull off when I came out?

I would have stood there thinking about it for much longer if I didn't remember that I had left the waffle maker cooking. Returning to my berry hunt and retrieving a few for breakfast, I scurried back to the kitchen and returned to my task.

No longer able to bask in the glow of the night before, I finished making breakfast with something else on my mind. Who had been parked out front? In truth, it could have been anybody. Maybe there someone due to check in today who I didn't know about. Maybe someone had gotten lost and had thought that that was a safe place to check their map.

The option that unsettled me was that it was someone from my past. C-Classes were common in my world. Could that have been the person who had run Dr. Sonya off the road thinking it was me? Had the danger I had put everyone in returned?

"They smell incredible," Cali said, making me jump.

"Oh man, you startled me."

"I'm sorry, Baby. What's got you so tense? I would have thought you'd be more relaxed after last night," he said with a smile.

I laughed at myself.

"I should be, right? By the way, is not being able to walk straight the next morning usual after being with you?"

Cali smiled again. "Want a massage to make it feel better," he said, wrapping his large hands around my ass.

"Probably. But don't you have to head out soon? I don't want you speeding to catch your class and getting into an accident."

Cali let me go and examined the plate I had prepared for him. Completing it with a smiley face made out of berries, I handed it to him.

"Aw. Thank you, Baby. It looks so good, I don't even want to eat it."

"Well, you have to. Because you need to tell me whether it's good enough to serve to your mother."

"However it tastes, I'm sure she'll love it."

"Thank you. But, seriously, tell me what you think. I might have added too much tamarind powder. And if I did, I will be making it again. Now, sit. Eat."

Sitting at the small table on the far side of the kitchen, he dug in.

"Mmmm. Baby, these are good!"

"You think so?" I asked nervously.

Before I could finish worrying about it, Cali finished the waffles and handed me the plate.

"It's the second-best thing I had all morning."

"The second best?" I asked confused.

"The best was when I had you in my arms," he said making me melt.

Cradling the back of my head in his hand, he lifted my chin and kissed my lips.

"I gotta run. But I'll be back as soon as I can to help with Mama. When that's done, do you think we could do more of what we did last night?"

"Sounds good to me," I said getting hard again thinking about it.

Watching him go was the hardest thing I had to do all morning. Actually, the hardest thing might have been walking, considering I still felt the imprint of his huge cock inside of me. I liked it, though. It reminded me of what we had done. It had all been worth the wait.

"No, you didn't," Dillon said, not believing me.

"I did," I confirmed, over the moon.

"Oh my God, Hil, I'm so proud of you. My boy is finally a man," he joked, feigning tears.

"By the way, why didn't you warn me about the morning after?"

Dillon became more serious. "What do you mean?"

"I can barely walk straight. You could have told me to expect that, Mr. *I've slept with a bunch of guys, so I have a lot of experience.*"

"What do you mean that you can't walk straight?"

"I mean that it hurts to walk."

"Wait, how big was he?"

Remembering that he had two fingers in me, I looked down at my hand and made a triangle with my middle finger on top.

"I don't know. Like, the width of three or four fingers. Hello? Dillon? Are you still there?"

"Hil, love you, but I officially hate you."

"What do you mean?"

"So, not only is the first guy you stumble upon the sweetest, nicest, most gorgeous guy ever, but he's so big that you can't walk straight the next day? How did you get so lucky?"

"Maybe I was saving it up after being unlucky for so long?"

"Well, whatever you do, do not screw this up. You may never find another guy like him," he warned me.

I felt a weight in my heart thinking about what I had to tell Dillon next.

"Speaking of screwing things up, I might have a problem?"

"What is it? That you've also won the lottery's jackpot after playing it for the first time?" he joked.

"No." I paused. "Did you tell Remy that you've heard from me?"

"No! You told me not to. And it's been very hard, by the way. He keeps calling me. You know I have a hard time not giving that man anything he wants whenever he looks at me."

"Again, eww. And I told you how important it is that you not mention anything about me. He has ways of making people talk. And you wouldn't like any of them."

"You keep making Remy seem like this bad guy. But I really don't think he is."

"Trust me, Dillon, you want to stay away from him. Everybody in my family is poison, including me."

"Don't say that, Hil. You're the greatest guy I know. I don't know where I would be without you.

You're basically my fairy godmother. No one would have done for me what you have."

"So, I hope you trust me when I say, stay away from him."

"Of course. Whatever you say. But what's all this about?"

"There was someone parked in front of the place this morning. When they saw me, they pulled off. I've never seen a car like that around before. I think someone might have tracked me here. And they might be the same person who ran my car off the road."

"Oh my God, Hil. You can't stay there."

"Where else am I supposed to go?"

"You can go home. I know you've been having fun, but someone tried to run you off the road and they could be back. Your life isn't worth some dick, no matter how big and fantastic it sounds."

"I'll think about it," I told Dillon, not knowing what else to say.

"Don't think about it, just go home. What if you're putting everyone there in danger?"

"What if I have and it's already too late to change things?" I said sadly.

"If you don't come home, I'm going to have to tell Remy where you are," Dillon said firmly.

"You can't."

"Why not? I would prefer you hate me than to lose you."

"Seriously, Dillon, don't. Please, don't. I'll take care of this. I promise. It could turn out to be a lost tourist. We could be freaking out over nothing."

"Don't make me have to call your brother for your own safety," Dillon said heartbroken.

"Promise me you won't."

"Promise me that you won't shut me out. I wouldn't be able to live with myself if something happens to you and I knew I could have done something about it."

"Just promise me you won't tell him. I can handle this. You need to have faith in me. Somebody does."

"I love you, Hil. I couldn't take losing you."

"You won't have to. I promise," I reassured him before wondering if what I had said was true.

Ending my call with Dillon, I couldn't stop thinking about what he had said. It was because of me that Dr. Sonya was confined to her bed. If, whoever it was, was still after me, what were they willing to do next?

Or, was all of this in my head? I had no way of knowing exactly what sent Dr. Sonya over the cliff. She mentioned being hit from behind. But couldn't it have been from someone joyriding the narrow mountain roads?

I hoped that was the case. It was hard living with the thought that I might have gotten someone killed. And, if they were still after me, what were they willing to do next? Would they go after someone else to get to me? Would someone else get in the way when they made another attempt on my life?

Needing to clear my mind, I left Dr. Sonya with everything she would need and then ran some errands. I didn't necessarily need to replenish the fridge. There was still a lot of food left. But I needed to get out into the fresh mountain air. I needed to get some distance on the matter to decide what I should do.

Climbing into the truck that I was beginning to enjoy driving, I drove the five minutes to the local grocery store. It was in the same parking lot as the diner. Heading in, I spotted Glen. He was the teddy-bear-looking brown skin guy who owned the place. I had met his husband, Dr. Tom, at the hospital the day of the accident. Although his husband seemed all business, Glen had to be the nicest guy in the world.

"Hil, how is Dr. Sonya doing? Tom told me that she's home from the hospital?" he asked turning his attention to me when I entered.

"She seems pretty good so far. She's definitely in high spirits."

Glen chuckled. "Yeah, that's her. I'm glad to hear she is doing better. Have you decided how long you'll be sticking around yet?" he said, referencing a conversation we had had when we first met.

"I don't know. This is a great town. It's easy to fall in love with the place. Everyone is so nice here," I told him not just thinking about Cali, but also his friends and Dr. Sonya.

"Well, the way I see it, you would be a wonderful addition to the community if you ever decided to stay. This town needs more young people like you. And, if you ever decided to attend university, I'm sure that Cali could show you around. It's a great school."

That was something I hadn't considered. Having been home schooled and coming from the family I had, attending university hadn't been an option. Beside it being too far outside of my father's protection, I hadn't received a formal education. According to public records, I hadn't even attended the 1st grade. I was a kindergarten dropout.

It wasn't that I didn't like learning. I did. I was allowed to direct my tutor in any direction I found interesting. Science had always fascinated me. But what was I going to do, become a doctor? There was no way my father would ever let me do anything as exposed as seeing patients.

Still, every day I spent with Cali working at the bed-and-breakfast, I gained more confidence in myself. I truly was capable of doing more than my father thought I could. Before now, I always hoped that was the case. Thanks to Cali, I knew I was capable of more.

Didn't that mean that I couldn't also attend university like a normal person? Even if I wanted to stay in this small town, couldn't I do what Cali was doing and commute?

I kept thinking about this as I mindlessly searched the aisles for anything we might need. Not finding inspiration, I looked back through the store's front glass and spotted something I hadn't expected to. Parked across the street and a distance away was the car I had seen when I went out for berries. It was black with tinted windows and nothing that would stop it from blending in on New York City streets.

"Have you seen that car around here before?" I asked Glen as my heart raced.

"Once or twice," Glen replied moving by my side. "Do you know him?"

"Have you seen who's driving it?"

"From a distance. Dark hair. A little intimidating looking if you ask me," he said with a smile. "We've been getting all types since the town has started showing up on maps. Usually, they're people like you or outdoorsy types looking for a tour of the waterfalls. That's what we're known for," Glen explained. "Not too many of them look like he did."

Continuing to stare at the car, I asked, "Have you ever seen the front of it?"

"Of what?"

"Of the car? Did you notice if there was any damage?"

Glen turned to me and stared with his mouth open.

"What are you suggesting?"

I looked at him wondering how much I could trust him with. He seemed like a great guy, but I decided that the less people who knew about me, the better.

"Nothing. I'm just being paranoid."

"You think that car might have been the one to run Dr. Sonya off the road?" Glen asked concerned.

"No. Like I said, I'm just being paranoid. Don't pay me any mind. I've been watched too many movies," I told him with a forced smile.

Looking at me like he didn't know what to believe, he eventually conceded and returned to checking the shelves. Deciding I didn't need anything from there, I said bye to Glen and headed towards the car to get a better look.

Staying on the opposite side of the street, it was locked in my gaze. I didn't want to take my eyes off of it. I couldn't see through the windows so I couldn't tell if anyone was in it. But if he was and was here to kill me, I wanted to see it coming.

Feeling my palms sweat, it became harder to breathe. My body crackled with fear and tension. And just as I was about to cross in front of it to see its front bumper, the car started up.

I froze. I had been an idiot. All he needed to do now was you turn and run into me. Exposed in the empty street, I had no escape.

Before I could move, the car shot off. Relief washed through me. I wouldn't die today. But I was sure that whoever had been in there, was here for me.

Watching it drive away, I saw my dreams of a simple life drive away with it. I had been right. Dr. Sonya had her accident because of me. I had put everyone in danger. I was either going to have to leave or…

Sitting in the kitchen, all I could think about was what I would do next. It was all over. The night before was now a distant memory. Cali was going to hate me. But what other choice did I have?

Hearing him drive up, I hurried to the living room's bay windows. Standing far enough so he couldn't see me, I watched him approach the front door. This was it. There was no turning back now.

"Hil," he said with a smile that lit my heart. "What's wrong?" he asked seeing me.

Tears filled my eyes. I wasn't able to move. He rushed to me putting his hands on my shoulders.

"What's wrong? Did something happen with Mama?" he said as terror filled him.

"No! She's fine," I quickly reassured him forgetting that that would be first place he would go.

"Everything's fine with her. She seemed to have a good day."

"Then, I don't understand. What's the matter?"

For as long as I had been thinking about it, I needed a moment to gather my thoughts.

"Do you know that feeling when you have to tell someone something, and you know that afterwards they'll never look at you the same again?"

"I don't know what's going on. But I promise you, there is nothing that you could say that would change the way I feel about you."

His kind words brought my forehead to his chest. He had made it harder for me to tell him what I had to. Gathering my courage, I looked into his eyes.

"There's something you don't know about me because I haven't told you."

"What's that?" he asked hesitantly.

"Do you know how I said that I was home schooled?"

"Yeah."

"There's a reason for that."

"Which is?"

I took a final breath before my life would change.

"I'm a part of a family."

Cali looked at me confused.

"Okay. So am I."

"No. I mean that my family is involved with things that aren't always legal," I told him as my skin burned.

He looked away and thought about it. His mouth dropped open when he understood.

"You mean that your family is in the mafia?"

I cringed hearing the word.

"We prefer to call it a family, but yes. That's what I'm saying."

Cali stared at me, not hinting to what he was thinking.

"Why are you telling me this now?"

"Because I think there's someone in town who was sent by a rival family. And I think he might be here to kill me."

Shock washed across Cali's face. He was a storm of emotions. When they settled, there was rage in his eyes. I thought it was directed towards me until…

"Hil, if anyone tried to hurt you, I swear to God I'll…"

"Stop, Cali. Please. Don't do anything to get yourself hurt. And, I can't be sure of this. There's just a car I saw parked out front which I again saw in town. It's suspicious. It freaked me out enough that I had to tell you."

"I'll keep you safe. I promise you that, Hil. You will be safe."

As much as what he said made me want him more, he had no idea what he would be up against. If this was a rival family's problem-solver, he wouldn't hesitate to kill the both of us. It was slowly dawning on me that I might have to protect Cali from himself.

"I think I need to go."

"No!" he said, grabbing me again. "I won't let you go. At least, not because of this. If you don't want anything else to do with me, I'll accept that. But I won't let anyone run you off. I'll fight with my last breath to have you with me."

"And that's what I'm afraid of," I explained softly.

When I said it, Cali caught himself. Letting go of me, he relented. Gathering strength from somewhere deep inside, he said, "I don't want you to go. I've had enough people I love leave me. I can't let you be another."

His words broke my heart. There was depth behind it from a source that I didn't yet know.

"And I don't wanna leave you. I wanna stay here and have countless nights like the one we had last night. All I want is to be with you."

"Then tell me how we should handle this. I trust you. I'll do anything you tell me as long as it means that we can be together."

Cali's vulnerability made my heart hurt. He really was the perfect guy. Dillon was right. I couldn't let him go. But at the same time, I needed to protect him.

"You also need to know that the person I saw might have been the one to run your mother off the road." "What?"

"I can't be sure. That's just a guess but it would make sense."

Cali looked away deep in thought. I grabbed his bicep, pressing my chest against his arm.

"You hate me, don't you?" I asked dreading the answer.

He spun towards me, gripping me in his large strong hands again.

"Never. I will never hate you."

"Then, what are you thinking?"

"That you might be wrong."

"What do you mean?"

"There's something I haven't told you. It's concerning my father."

"What about him?"

"He might have been the one who ran my mother off the road. She won't say why. And she can't be sure either. But she seems to think it's a possibility."

I stared at Cali not knowing what to think. I was having a problem formulating words.

"Do you hate me now?" Cali asked, flipping the script.

"Of course not. It's just that…"

"What?"

"I think you're wrong."

"But, what if I'm not? Would you still need to leave?"

I pulled away from him thinking about that. I hadn't considered that the accident was because someone was trying to kill Dr. Sonya. The idea seemed inconceivable. Who would want to hurt someone like her?

"Do you still think you need to leave?" Cali asked drawing my attention.

"No," I told him, surprising myself. "I'm not afraid of your father, whoever he is. I won't run from being with you. I'm falling for you hard, Cali."

Cali pulled me to him, sweeping me into his arms.

"And I've fallen for you," he said bringing tears to my eyes.

Chapter 10

Cali

As the scenery rushed by me on my way back to campus, all I could think about was Hil. I wasn't going to lose him. I would fight with my last breath to keep him. I wasn't yet sure what that meant. But I was going to figure it out.

Remembering the feel of his soft skin under my fingertips, I felt a rush. The angles of his lean body gliding against my palm made me feel alive. He was someone I would run into a burning building to save. I would blindly jump off a cliff for him. And when I pictured his naked body again, I had to adjust my hardening cock as it fought against my jeans.

Lost in the thought of him, I was ripped back to earth when my phone rang. My first thought was that it was Hil. Scrambling to answer it, I glanced at the caller ID. It rocked me to my core.

"Dr. Tom, what is it?" I asked with a knot tightening in my stomach.

"Cali, I have some news about your mother's situation. There was something on your her x-ray that looked unusual to me, so I forwarded it to a few specialists. It turns out that the surgery I discussed with you should be done as soon as we can schedule her."

Blood rushed out of my face hearing his words.

"Why? What's the matter?"

"It's nothing that you need to be overly concerned about. It's just that the longer we wait, the less her chances are of making a full recovery."

"So you're saying that if she doesn't have the surgery soon, she might not be able to walk again?"

"Think of it more as, the longer we postpone the surgery, the lower her quality of life will be."

"That's serious."

"Only if we put it off for too long. So, when can I schedule her in for the procedure?"

I wasn't prepared for this. He had said that because we didn't have insurance, the hospital was going to make us prove that we had the ability to pay. We didn't have that type of money and I had no idea how I could get it.

"Can I get back to you on that?"

"Absolutely. But, remember, the longer you wait, the harder it will be for her to return to being the person she used to."

Ending the call with Dr. Tom, I entered a daze. Where was I going to get that type of money? We barely had a bank in Snow Tip Falls. I didn't know where to begin.

Distracted during all of my classes, I didn't have it in me to drive back home. I didn't know how I was going to tell any of this to my mother.

Growing up, it had just been the two of us. I was the man of the house before I even knew what that meant. But I had always done my best to take care of my mother. How was I going to take care of her with this?

"Okay, Cali, what's up?" Titus asked from his desk in our dorm room.

I continued staring at the ceiling as I asked, "What do you mean?"

"First of all, you're here," he said adjusting his chair to face me. "Weren't you excited about Hil? Why are you here instead of with him?"

"Is Lou coming over?" I asked about his boyfriend.

"I'm not trying to get rid of you. I'm asking because you seem even quieter than normal. And that's saying a lot."

I turned towards him finding his usual half-smile. I knew he was only trying to be my big brother, and I appreciated him for that. But I wasn't sure what to say.

"You know you can talk to me about anything, right? Even about Hil," he said sincerely.

I thought about that.

"I think our father tried to kill my mother," I told him, relieving one of the weights from my shoulders.

"What?" he exclaimed shocked. "Why would you say that? What happened?"

I opened my mouth to speak before he stopped me.

"Wait, let me call Claude. We're brothers. We should be talking about this together."

As he retrieved his phone and called Claude, I considered stopping him. I wasn't sure if this was something that should stay between the two of us. But Claude was my brother as much as Titus was. He had as much right hearing this as Titus or I did.

"Hey, what's up?" Claude said from the other end of the FaceTime.

"Cali thinks it was our father who ran his mother off the road," Titus explained.

"Seriously? Why?"

"He was about to tell me. I thought I should loop you in."

"I appreciate it. What's going on Cali? Why do you think our father tried to kill your mother?"

I sat up, facing the two of them. "It's not me who's saying it, it's Mama. And she didn't say that she thought it was him, specifically. She implied that our father might have gotten someone to do it."

"Do you mean like he was some sort of gangster?" Titus asked. "Is she hinting something about our father?"

I looked at Titus. "He would have to be someone who has the money and the connections to do it. And, if he did, and it's still an *if*, the guy he hired might be back in town to finish the job."

"Whoa," Titus exclaimed.

"Why are you saying that?" Claude asked.

"Hil said that yesterday morning there was someone parked out in front of our place. He then saw them again when he was shopping at Glen's."

Claude clarified, "And you think this is the person who ran your mother off the road?"

"It could be."

"How do we find out for sure?" Claude asked, being the logical, practical person that he was.

I looked at Titus.

"What are you looking at me for? I don't know anything about this."

"We're looking at you because you're the closest thing our town has to a mayor," Claude explained.

"What are you talking about? No one's elected me."

"Not yet. But elections are coming up. The town incorporated because you made it happen. Everyone trusts you. Who do you think people gonna vote for to lead us through the transition?" Claude clarified.

"He's right," I added.

Titus's gaze bounced between the two of us. He knew it was true.

"Even if that was the case, I'm not the mayor now. And, what am I supposed to do about it even if I was?"

"Appoint someone to look into this," Claude said.

"You mean like a sheriff, another elected position?"

"A temporary sheriff," I pointed out.

"So you're saying that I should take the authority that I don't have and appoint someone to a position that I have no right to?"

"Being a leader is hard. And we need someone to look into this," Claude told him.

"Who would I even appoint?" Titus asked flustered.

I thought for a moment.

"What about Cage?"

"As sheriff?" Titus questioned.

"I could see that," Claude agreed.

Titus thought about that. "Do you think Quin would be okay with his boyfriend doing something so dangerous?"

"It's for the greater good," Claude decided.

"Yeah, but…"

"Doesn't Cage already seem like a sheriff," I joked. "Couldn't you see him in that uniform?"

Although all of us had played football, Cage was the only one who had the physique of a fitness model. I had Hil, but that didn't stop me from imagining how good Cage would look in a uniform.

"Maybe," Titus conceded. "I can call him and ask him if he has any ideas on what to do."

Claude sighed.

"There might be something I can do, as well. I have been hesitant to ask my mother for details about our father. For my whole life, it felt like a topic she didn't want to talk about. And after I saw the way your mothers responded when you two asked them, I decided not to bring it up with her. Maybe it's time I did," he said solemnly.

"Okay. I'll talk to Cage, and you talk to your mother. Meanwhile, Cali, maybe you should see what else your mother will tell you. I can't imagine she'd be willing to keep secrets if people's lives are on the line. How about we talk again when one us has more information?"

"Will do," Claude agreed.

"Yeah," I said, unsure if I would be able to hold up my end of the agreement. I didn't know if that was something my mother would want to talk about now, considering everything else that was going on.

How was I going to tell her that she needed to go into surgery as soon as possible if I didn't know where to find the money for it? I couldn't let her down. There had to be something I could do to earn the cash. But it was a lot, and I needed the money fast.

Knowing that I couldn't stay out all night, I drove back thinking about everything we had discussed as I did. Stepping through the door, the sight of Hil relaxed me. On top of that, he had made me dinner.

"You're becoming quite the chef," I told him, meaning it.

"I'm so glad you liked it. Your mother said that that was your favorite. I was hoping you would get back before it got cold," he said vulnerably.

I lowered my head thinking about why it was I was late. There was so much going on. There were so many things I needed to talk about. Life was becoming overwhelming until Hil reached across the table and took my hand. Looking into his eyes, he didn't say a word. But what I couldn't miss was his empathy. It made me love him more.

Lifting his hand to my lips, I kissed it. It was like nectar. I needed to kiss it again. Leaning towards me, he rested his small hand against my jawline. Putting my hand on his, I kissed the heel of his palm and then his wrist.

That was when the dam broke. Feeling his soft skin against mine, I needed more. Pressing the inside of my arm against the outside of his, I leaned forward delivering a trail of kisses. When I couldn't go any further, I clutched my fingers in his. I could barely breathe. He was my air.

"I need you," I told him, feeling it deep inside. "I burn for you. Without you, I can barely see straight. Every room I enter, I'm looking for you," I told him, meaning every word.

"I need you too," he said with near tears in his eyes.

That was all it took. Sweeping everything off the table between us, I climbed across it not letting anything stop me from being with him.

As he stood up, I rushed towards him. Protecting him in my arms, we hit the wall with a thump. Finding his lips, I consumed him. He was a fine berry, and I devoured him.

His lips, his tongue, the apple of his cheeks, his ear, I wanted to taste all of him. So, slipping my hand between his shirt and flesh, I pulled it off of him. Finding the creamy tones of his neck and then his clavicle, I hurt with passion.

I loved touching him. I loved being able to touch him. Tracing a path down his lean chest, I found his nipple. Nibbling it, I pulled. He moaned, tortured by my desire. But wrapping my arms around him and burying my fingertips deep into his flesh, he grabbed my hair and pulled me tighter to him.

Needing more, I continued down. Finding the valley of his abs, I held both of his sides in my hands. Hil was so small compared to me. I was like a monster. But kissing him and holding him, I was subdued until all that was left was his jeans and my lust.

Shifting my hands to his ass, I pressed his hard cock against my face. His outline was clear through the fabric. As small as the rest of him was, his manhood was not. This was now a part of him I needed in my mouth. And hungrier than I had ever been, I tore at his button and then zipper until there was nothing separating me from his beautiful throbbing flesh.

Cradling his balls, I leaned towards it. I savored his taste like a fine alcohol. Wanting it but not wanting the moment to end, I approached it with the tip of my nose. Inhaling him as I explored his length, my craving became too much.

Throwing myself onto him, I pushed the tip of his cock into my throat.

"Ahhh!" he squealed, throwing his palms onto the wall behind him.

I wanted more of that. I wanted to hear him beg for relief from pleasure. I wanted him to feel more joy than he had ever in his life. So, gripping his balls and shining his head with my tongue, I pushed him into me until like a kettle, his whistle blew.

His cum tasted like lemongrass. It was incredible. Drinking every drop he had to offer, I didn't let him go until he placed his hand on my head, begging for me to stop.

Kneeling before him, I panted like an animal. I was crazed for him. I didn't know what to do with myself. He had tamed me, and I sat waiting like a good pup. But waiting for that signal, I was ready to attack. His manhood raised and lowered with his breaths. His lean, flat body was majestic. His face was that of an angel.

When his desperate eyes opened and look down at me needing more, he didn't have to say a word. Lifting his pants and scooping him into my arms, I carried him through the living room and up the stairs. Kicking open my bedroom door, I found the bed. Giving us the privacy we would need, I looked down at him slowly removing my clothes.

Was it craving or fear that filled his eyes? Was it both? I couldn't tell, but everything about him wanted me. His pose, his again rigid cock. He laid beneath me wanting me to take him. That is exactly what I did.

Lowering his toes to his ears, I positioned my covered, lubed dick. Entering him, he moaned. It was guttural. The rumble began at his sex.

Resting the back of his legs onto my chest, I leaned down and kissed him. I needed to keep kissing him. How many ways could I find to be inside of him? He was all I ever wanted and all I would ever need. So, when the slapping of my deep strokes reached his button and he again sprayed, this time onto his own face, I curled my back and howled at the moon.

I would have filled him to the brim if not for the latex between us. Instead, I lowered his legs and relaxed on top of him. With the flat of his feet on the mattress, I was still inside of him. I was still hard and his small size didn't want to let me go.

Knowing that I would stay erect as long as I was buried in his hole, I shifted my hip slowly trying to ease out. It was then that I remembered how big I was. I never wanted to hurt him.

"I'm sorry," I whispered, saying it over and over.

"I love you," he whispered back, taking a warm hold of my heart.

Needing to catch my breath a little longer, we relaxed with me still in him. Wanting us to be even closer, he wrapped his legs around my hips and I slipped my hands behind his back. We felt as one. We moved as one. And when Hil was ready to let me go, my cock slid out.

That didn't end the embrace we had on each other, though. Burying his small body into my chest, it was there that he fell asleep. I didn't know how I had gotten so lucky to find someone like this. But there was no way I was ever going to let him go. I knew that I couldn't even if I tried. So, what was I going to do now?

Chapter 11

Hil

I'm losing myself to him. Laying in his arms, I don't know where I end and where he begins. With his chest pressed against my back, our hearts beat as one.

I could never have imagined that being with someone could feel like this. The thought of him letting me go hurt. I would do anything to live in this moment.

But even as I lay there a voice whispered in the back of my mind. It told me that Cali had been wrong about who the driver of the Mercedes was. Yes, it might have been his father like he had thought. But how could it not be someone sent by a rival family to seek revenge on all of my father's past deeds?

Growing up, I knew who my father was. He was the most kind and loving man a son could ask for. His greatest crime towards me was too desperately wanting to help me. It's didn't work out the way he had hoped. But I know he never meant to be cruel.

That, however, was not how he dealt with others. Remy made sure that I knew that. The stories my brother told me about my father's cruelties kept me up at night. How could the man who held me and watched over me the way he did, also carry out the crimes Remy described? He made our father seem like a madman. What part of my father was inside of me?

There was definitely a part of my father in Remy. He and I were nothing alike. The reason my father gave my brother the freedom that he had was because no one dared to mess with him. Did Remy have my father's sadistic cruelty? Not that I saw. But I didn't see it in Father either.

Do Remy's sleeve tattoos paint the picture I should have of my brother? They were so much like my father's. And the way Remy looked at people, it was like he was staring straight through them. At times, I wondered how many people would survive if Remy had an axe. I came from a family of bad men. How could I ever inflict that on Cali?

"I love you," I said, unsure if he was awake to hear it.

"I love you too," he said tightening his grip on me.

I couldn't do this. Not to him. To be with him would be to betray him. I had already gotten one person hurt. Who would be next? If I loved him, I had to leave him.

"Cali, I…"

I paused. I had to say it but I couldn't.

"Tell me something you've never told anybody," I said to him instead.

Cali didn't speak. When the silence drew out, I wondered if he had heard me. With his arms holding me tighter, I knew there was something wrong. Forcing my way out of his arms, I rolled over and looked at him. His eyes were lowered. What had I said?

"What's the matter?" I asked him.

"There's something going on that I can't fix," he said, eventually breaking his silence.

I placed my palm on his chest, aching from his pain.

"Whatever it is, you can tell me. Please, let me in," I told him, ready to beg.

As soon as I asked, he pulled himself together.

"It's nothing. I'll handle it. I'll figure out a way."

"Don't do that. My father does that. He solves problems and the way he does it…," I said losing myself to Remy's stories. "If you care about me, I need to believe that you trust me enough to help. I'm not weak or a burden. I need you to think more of me than that. I can't take you seeing me that way as well.

"Someone has to see me as worth something. If it isn't you, I don't know who it will be," I said for the first time touching the depth of my pain.

"You're right. I can trust you. You've done more for me in the short time I've known you then people I've known my whole life. If there's anyone I can trust, it's you."

"Then tell me. Maybe I can help. At least give me that chance."

Cali's gaze washed over me before drifting away. It took a moment, but eventually he said, "My mother needs surgery."

"Oh no," I said feeling his pain.

"It's okay. Dr. Tom tells me it's not a complex procedure. She just needs it as soon as I can afford to pay it."

"That's great."

"Except, I can't afford it. I haven't told my mother, but I know what's in her bank account. She can't afford it either.

"Is that it? Are you just worried about the money?"

"Money's a big deal. I don't know what it's like to grow up in a penthouse in New York City. But here in Snow Tip Falls, money doesn't grow on trees."

I could see Cali's frustration, and he was right. It was my crazy upbringing that made me think that something like this wasn't what the rest of the world fought over. Wasn't money what drove my father to do the things I was told he did?

"I didn't mean it like that," I told him apologetically. "It's just that I have money."

"And that's great for you—"

"No, I mean I have cash. I brought it with me."

"That's very nice of you. But the surgery will cost thousands of dollars."

"And that's what I brought. Whatever you need, I can give you. And if I don't have it on me, there are ways I can get it."

"I know you're trying to be nice by saying that. But I can't take your money."

"Why not? Besides, it's not my money. I mean, it's my money, but you wouldn't be taking it from me. You would be putting it to use in a way that helps people.

"I want to help you. I think I need to help you. Your mother might be in the situation she is because of me. If I can fix that by giving you a bunch of paper from the trunk of my car, you've got to let me do it," I told him, feeling desperate.

"Hil…"

"Cali, please. Really, please," I said, realizing I wouldn't be able to take it if he said no.

He must have seen my sincerity. Or, maybe he was just feeling sorry for me. Because without being able to look me in the eyes, he nodded his head, agreeing to let me give it to him.

"Thank you! You don't know how much this means to me," I said again. "Now, there's only one problem."

"What's that?"

"I have it. I brought it with me. But…"

"You don't have it with you?"

"It's at the bottom of the ravine in the trunk of my car."

Cali thought about it for a moment.

"Wait, you have thousands of dollars in the trunk of your car?"

"Yeah."

"Were you just planning on leaving it there?"

"It's not like I could have gone and gotten it," I explained.

"Wait, you were really just going to leave thousands of dollars there. You never thought to go back and get it?"

"I mean, I considered it. But I saw the pictures. Your mother had to be helicoptered out of there. How is someone supposed to go down there to get it?"

"You hike," Cali said, as if it was the most obvious thing in the world.

"From where?"

"From wherever we need to," he said, still leaving me confused.

"Well, if you can get to it, like I said, it's yours."

"We can get to it."

"We? I think you're overestimating the skills of this city boy," I explained.

"No, you can do it. We both can. We just need a little rope, a couple of harnesses, and maybe rash guards to protect our arms from the branches as we lower ourselves. But we can do it," he said with a long, absent smile.

It took a day of studying the images from Google Maps for us to come up with a game plan. He was treating it like a football game. His brother, who had a company giving adventure tours to tourists, had all the equipment we needed. So, when we woke up the morning we planned to go, I felt nervous but well prepared.

Driving to the site of the accident, neither of us said much. Cali because, well, he's Cali. And me because I still thought of it as the place I almost got his mother killed.

It meant so much to me that he was allowing me to make amends for what I had done. I wasn't my father or brother. I couldn't hurt people and then shake it off. I needed to balance the scales and make things right.

"We're here," I announced as he pulled the truck onto the side of the road. I was hoping it would make me feel less nervous. It didn't.

"You can do this," he said, seeing how I felt.

"I'll believe you when I see it," I joked.

Seeing the skid marks on the road, I walked to where they ended. It made me dizzy just to stand there. There were no rails to hold on to. With a strong breeze, I would have been thrown to my death.

Bracing myself, I looked down. There it was, my car. It was hard to believe that Dr. Sonya had survived that. Thank you, German engineering. Having landed front first, the car was ass up. It looked intact and accessible. If we could get down there, Cali's plan could work.

Taking a deep breath, I shifted my attention to the horizon. The car was at the top of a hill but, in total, we had to be 400 feet in the air. The trees around us stretched out for miles. I couldn't imagine how long it would take to go the long way around if we had to. The direct approach really was our best option.

"I still don't get it. How are we supposed to get down there?" I asked him again.

"We're going to tie this rope onto an anchor, maybe a tree trunk or a large rock, and then lower ourselves down."

"And how are we going to do that?"

He held up a metal device that looked like a teardrop that was the size of his palm.

"This is called a GriGri. When you pull this lever," he said touching it with his thumb, "It will lower you. When you let it go, it acts like a break. So if you panic, just remember to let it go. You'll be safe."

"If I panic, I'll be more concerned about falling to my death to remember your instructions."

"That's fine. Just remember, when you fall to your death, stretch out your arms. Treat it like a roller coaster. It's important," he said with a hint of a smile.

"Wait, are you making jokes. You choose now to start making jokes?"

"If you throw out your arms, you'll release the switch. I'm trying to get you not to die," he clarified.

Staring at him, I walked to him and gave him a kiss. "And that's why I'm crazy about you," I said again feeling safe.

"Wanting you not to die seems like a pretty low bar, but low standards are where I thrive."

I stared at him again. He really was trying to be funny at a time like this. I mean, it was adorable and making me a little hard, but still, timing.

Feeling a bit more relaxed, I listened intently as Cali described how to put on the harness. It was pretty simple. So was lowering oneself. When he was done, I genuinely believed that I could do it.

Deciding to anchor the rope on his truck's hitch, he tossed the length of it into the ravine. It was just long enough to reach the car. Everything seemed good until I asked him, "How are we supposed to get back up?"

He gave me a devilish smile as if I caught him trying to get away with something.

"That one is just a matter of hard work. There are two things we can do. We won't know which one is better until we get there. We could either tie into the rope and rock climb our way out. It will be safe but it probably won't be easy. Or, we can hike around."

"Do you mean, hike around the mountain?" I clarified.

He nodded.

"Okay. Now that you've established that there are no good options, I will proceed to latch myself onto the rope and lower myself to my death. It was nice knowing you," I said before attaching my GriGri and doing what I had been taught.

I had to admit, as terrifying as it was, it was also kind of fun. I had seen people repel down cliffs in movies. Now here I was doing it. I couldn't even imagine something like this a few weeks ago. I had never felt more alive.

Approaching the ground before Cali, I looked into the car's cabin. All of the airbags had deployed. Mixed in within the deflated fabric were the glass shards from the windshield. There was also blood, Dr. Sonya's blood. I wondered if Cali needed to see this. It was just a reminder of why I shouldn't be anywhere near him.

When Cali detached himself and joined me by my side, I was overcome with guilt.

"This was not your fault," he said, reading me like a book. "We don't know who's responsible for this and to say one way or another would just be a guess. The only thing we can say for sure is that you weren't driving the car that hit her. And we'll figure out who was. I promise. I already have my brothers working on it," he said, putting his hand on my shoulder massaging it.

"You're right. You're always right," I said wrapping my arms around him and lacing my fingers behind his back. I held him for a while until saying, "By the way, should I have brought my car keys for the trunk?"

I pulled away and looked up into his eyes. His mouth was open, but he couldn't speak. It was like his brain was on reset.

"What?"

"Should I have brought the keys?" I asked again, sustaining the joke as long as I could.

I laughed.

"Who's making jokes now?" Cali teased.

I pulled the car's key fob out of my pocket and held it into the air as I push the button for the trunk. It popped open. Seriously, German engineering.

With it open, Cali figured out a way up to it. Although sticking ass up, the back of the car rested on the side of the cliff. It would take a lot for it to dislodge and even more for the ground beneath it to give way to the flatland a few 100 feet below.

Using our rope as support, Cali climbed up the top of the car until he was staring into the trunk.

"Wow! You weren't kidding. You really do have stacks of cash just sitting in your trunk," he confirmed looking into the cabin. "Wait, what's that?" he asked, looking confused.

"What's what?"

He looked into the trunk at a loss for words.

"I don't know how to describe it. Come take a look."

Taking a deep breath to find my courage, I grabbed on to the end of the rope and climbed to the top of the car. Feeling as though I would fall at any moment, I death-gripped the only thing keeping me from my doom as I stared down into the trunk.

"What are you talking about?" I asked, not seeing much past the blinding fear.

Cali pointed.

"There. That's the cash. But what's that?"

I pulled myself together and followed his gaze. What I saw confused me. When I took the car and had packed it, the trunk was empty. Now there was something in it that looked like wiring and a computer's motherboard wrapped around a brick of clay. What was it? How did it get there?

When the answer hit me, it was like fire roared through me.

"Oh, shit! Quick! Get the fuck out of here!"

Panicked, Cali asked, "What's the matter?"

"It's a fucking bomb!" Recognizing a bomb was the only other thing my father had taught me. "This is what a bomb looks like. Quick, go!" I said before pushing him, giving him no choice.

As he fell to the ground below, I shouted, "Run!" As he scrambled to his feet, I climbed into the trunk to get the cash.

"What are you doing?" he yelled up after me.

"Just run," I told him, retrieving the money and then trying to figure out how to get out.

"If it's a bomb, I'm not leaving without you."

"I'm right behind you. Seriously you need to get out of here."

"Not without you!" he demanded.

It wasn't like I needed more convincing, but knowing that I was putting him at risk the longer I stuck around, I tossed the bundle and fought my way out of what was a respectfully deep trunk. I tell you, German engineering, I thought gripping the outer rim as I climbed.

Scratching and fighting, I pulled my way to the top and threw myself past the car. Expecting to hit the ground, I fell into Cali's arms. Once again, he had protected me. I would think about that later. Right now, we seriously needed to go.

With him following me down the hill the car sat on, neither of us spoke. We just scrambled down. 50 feet from the flat ground, I considered whether I had gotten it wrong. Had what I seen been a bomb? It certainly looked like one. But that didn't make sense. Why would there be an activated bomb in my trunk?

Stepping onto the soil scattered on the mountainous rock, I slowed to a stop.

"What?" Cali said still in a panic.

"Why hasn't it exploded?"

"Shouldn't we consider that when we are at a safe distance?"

Thinking about it again, I stared up from where we had come from. Nothing was happening. There was no explosion and no rocks falling down. By getting us to run, the only thing I had done was put us further from the rope we needed to climb our way out. Oh no, I had really screwed up.

Realizing it, I slowly turned to Cali. How was I going to make this up to him? It was gonna take us another hour to climb back up to the rope we needed to climb back up to the truck. With the pain of remorse filling me, I looked into Cali's worried eyes and said,

"I think I fucked up." And then the bomb exploded.

The sound was deafening. The echo from the cliff face repeated it and bore the noise to the base of our brains. Dropping to the ground involuntarily, we next had to dodge the falling rocks and debris.

This wasn't just a firecracker. The bomb tore the car apart. Hurrying to our feet, we ran through the trees as fast as we could. We didn't know what would be rolling down the hill after us, but we needed to be as far away from it as we could be if we were going to survive.

Zigzagging between the trees as we fled for our lives, we didn't stop until we were sure that we were far enough that nothing would get us. Leaning over with our hands on our knees, we fought for breath. Cali, who still had the money locked under his arm, stared at me bewildered.

There was no longer a question who had run Dr. Sonya off the road. I didn't know anything about Cali's father. But, whoever he was, would have had no reason to place a bomb in my trunk.

Chapter 12

Cali

"Why?" I asked Hil, not understanding anything about what was going on.

"He had to have climbed down to have confirmed that I was in the car when it went off the cliff. To get paid, he would have needed proof of death. A picture, something. When he couldn't get it, he must have searched the trunk and found the money."

"Are you saying that the guy who did this was a professional? Like, he did this for a living?"

"Yeah. Families hire people to take care of things like this," he said, giving me a glimpse of what his world was truly like.

I searched the ground, trying to make sense of what I was hearing.

"But, why not just take the money and be done with it? There's a lot here," I said, showing it to him.

Staring at me with sadness, Hil explained.

"He wouldn't have done that because, first off, he doesn't know if the money has been cleaned. If he took it and spent it, it could have shown up on some government agency's watch list. If the money hasn't been washed, it's basically kindling.

"Secondly, you might think that's a lot of money, but in my world, it's not. I was able to take that from my father because our place is exploding with it. Banks aren't a thing where I come from. So, when you're as successful as my father is, you have more cash sitting around than you can keep track of."

I was finally getting it. Hil was not like me. The world he grew up in was as similar to mine as a grape was to a river.

I didn't care, though. Whoever he was, wherever he came from, he was here now, and this was the man I loved. More important, there was someone who was trying to hurt my baby. That was never going to happen. I would tear this world apart trying to find this guy. And when I did, he would never get the chance to hurt Hil again.

It was a long way back around the mountain to the main road. As we walked everything about me was on alert. I was carrying thousands of dollars in cash while checking behind every tree for the person who had set the bomb. He might have been waiting for us.

When Hil spoke, I didn't answer. I couldn't focus on keeping him safe if I was thinking about anything else. It was my job to protect him. I was going to do it even if it required every moment of my waking life.

Eventually reaching the road, we also gained service on our phones. My first call was to the town's soon to be mayor, Titus.

"I don't think it was our father. There was a bomb in the trunk of Hil's car."

"There was a bomb?" Titus asked shocked.

"A bomb! And it almost killed us."

"We should call the county police or something."

"What's the county police gonna do?"

"Don't call the police!" Hil said, grabbing my arm.

Putting my hand over the phone, I asked, "Why not?"

"I told you what my father does. If you tell the police, they're gonna have to call the FBI. The last thing my family needs are Feds asking questions about us."

I stared at Hil realizing how insane all of this was. It wasn't like I would trust his protection with anyone else. But the fact that going through official channels wasn't even an option was mind blowing.

"Are you going to call your father?" I asked, knowing that if he did, he would be taken away from me.

Hil lowered his head.

"Not if I can help it," he said sadly.

Seeing his pain hardened my resolve. We were going to take care of this locally. We didn't need the police or Hil's father to come in and do what we could without their help.

Turning my attention back to the call, I said,

"Titus, we need to find the guy in the Mercedes. I want whoever you can find to be at my place as soon as they can get there. We need protection parked outside. We need people patrolling. And we need this guy caught and taken care of."

"I don't know about this, Cali," Titus said softening.

"I've never asked you for anything. Nothing. And except for this, I never will. You want to prove to me that we're brothers? Do this for me. I would do it for you."

It took Titus a moment to respond, but he did.

"Okay. We'll find this guy. But you realize that someone might get hurt?"

"I'm counting on it, Titus. But it won't be any of us. Let's just find him."

Walking back to the truck, I had a singular focus. In my mind, I went over every person in town the stranger could be staying with and every place his car could be parked when it wasn't parked outside our place.

Did the current guests have anything to do with this? No, probably not. This had to be someone from

New York. A man who knew how to rig a bomb wasn't someone who could easily blend in as an eco-tourist at a bed-and-breakfast.

Back at the truck, I retrieved Titus's rope, removed our climbing gear, and then drove us back to my place. I could barely focus on the road ahead of us. I had to search every corner and pull-off on the way.

"Cali, are you listening to me?" I eventually heard Hil say.

"What? Yeah, of course I'm listening. What did you say?" I said with my eyes still scanning everything around us.

"I said that I'm not sure about what you're doing," Hil repeated.

"What do you mean? I promise you; we will have every available person looking for this guy. No one's gonna get to you. You'll be as safe as you would be if your father was looking after you," I reassured him.

"That's what I'm afraid of," he said without further explanation.

"What do you mean?"

"Nothing," he said softly before staring out the window.

"Hil, you know I'll keep you safe, right?" I asked, knowing that I hadn't yet earned his trust.

"I know," he said without looking at me.

I continued to stare at him. I didn't understand what was going on. Maybe I should have pushed him to tell me what he was thinking, but there were more important things happening. If I let my guard down for a moment, I wasn't sure what would happen. I needed to focus on getting him back home and safe. That was the only thing that mattered right now.

Pulling up to the bed-and-breakfast, I spotted Claude's truck. As soon as I parked, Claude came outside to greet me.

"Titus called me. He told me what happened. Are you two alright?" he asked with a steely look and a crinkle between his eyes.

Still scanning our surroundings, I exited the truck and shielded Hil with my body as I escorted him inside. Under my arm was the money. The plastic it was wrapped in didn't hide what it was. After examining us, Claude's eyes fell to it.

"We're both fine. But there's someone out there, and we need to find him," I explained, capturing Claude's attention.

"Do we have a plan yet?" he asked.

"We need one person to keep a lookout here. And we need at least one car, maybe two out looking for him."

"If he's setting bombs, he's definitely armed. I'm not much with a gun, but I can make sure there's no one driving up. I can keep watch out front," he volunteered.

"Thank you. I appreciate that," I told him.

The creases in his beautiful brown skin softened.

"We have your back. Whatever you need, we'll be here for you. We'll find the guy," he said, reassuring me.

Leaving me, Claude returned to his truck. With him watching the road, I secured the money in my closet and checked in on Hil. I wasn't sure how to interpret what I saw in him. He wasn't nearly as concerned as I was.

Was it that he trusted me to handle it? I hoped so. But it might have been that he was frustrated. About what? I was doing everything I could to keep him safe. Would his father have done more?

When Cage arrived, I explained the situation again. He acted like the sheriff my brothers and I thought he would be.

"I can drive up to the site and take a look around. Maybe there's something there that could give us a clue to where he is," he explained. "I really think we should call someone, though. Someone set a bomb. This is a matter for the FBI."

"You can't," Hil said from behind me on the couch.

"That's not an option," I told Cage. "We have to handle this."

"A lot of things could go bad if we take care of this ourselves," Cage told me.

"Those things have already gone bad. Someone tried to kill us. Someone ran my mother off the road. We need to stop him. If you're not willing to do what's necessary, tell me. I will. You just find him, and I'll take care of the rest," I said staring into his eyes.

Seeing that I was serious, Cage didn't object. He nodded and then exited for his truck.

"Cali," Hil said, drawing my attention.

There was sadness in his eyes. It hurt to see. I needed him to know that everything was going to be alright. He was going to be alright. How could I get him to see that?

"Hil, you don't have to worry," I explained to him. "I will take care of you," I told him, slipping his hands in mine.

Hil's eyes dipped.

"What is it?"

"Nothing," he told me again.

There was something about the way he was acting that made me uneasy.

"If there's something wrong, you have to tell me. I can't take care of it if you don't tell me," I insisted.

Hil looked up into my eyes. He looked so vulnerable. It broke my heart.

"I love you, Cali," he told me.

Warmth rippled through my body.

"I love you too, Hil. And, don't worry. I have you," I reassured him again.

Cage's visit was followed by Bill from the diner, Marcus, and eventually Titus. Everyone was there to do whatever they could. Marcus agreed to exchange shifts with Claude while Bill and Titus patrolled the town.

Titus also agreed to recruit others. People like Glen would be able to keep watch from where they worked. My brother said he would get the whole town involved if necessary.

By the time night fell, I felt confident that we had this. There was still no way I would let down my guard, but we were going to be able to keep Hil safe. I was sure of it.

Chapter 13

Hil

Rolling over in bed, I reached for Cali. He wasn't there. I had become so used to feeling him next to me, his absence woke me up.

Opening my eyes, I looked around. I was in his bedroom, and it was dark. The clock on the night stand said it was 3:00 AM. Where was he?

It had been a week since finding the bomb. I had hoped that everything would have blown over by now. It hadn't. And Cali's obsession to keep me safe had gotten worse.

Guessing where he was, I pulled on a pair of shorts and headed to the living room. The creaky stairs drew Cali's attention. It was dark, but his profile was illuminated by the moonlight. Although I couldn't see them, I felt his concerned eyes on me.

"I woke up and you weren't there," I told him sadly.

"No one was able to be on watch tonight," he explained.

"So, you're doing it?"

Cali didn't respond. He didn't have to.

Crossing the distance between us, I sat in front of him and crawled into his arms. He held me as we both stared through the bay window.

"How long is this going to go on?" I asked him kindly.

"We'll find him. There are only so many places he could be hiding if he's here. If he isn't, he'll definitely be back. When he gets here, we'll stop him."

"But what if he doesn't come back? Will this be our life? I don't wanna do this to you."

"You're not doing anything to me. What are you talking about?"

"I'm talking about this. You can't sleep because you're so worried about me. And you have every guy in town out looking for someone who might never come back. I've turned your life upside down."

"You're not doing anything to me. I'm here because I wanna be. I want you to know that you can feel safe here. That's why we're all doing it."

"And I appreciate it. I really do. But at what cost?"

"Hil, I would pay any cost to be with you. Know that," he said, tightening his grip and touching his chin to my temple.

I loved the feeling of being in his arms. There was nowhere else I preferred to be. I couldn't imagine being happier than I was when I was with Cali. He was everything to me.

But how could I be this person for him? I had made his life so much worse. Before I had come, he wasn't up at three o'clock in the morning staring out of the window waiting for someone who may never come. The town wasn't out patrolling the streets. I had done that to them. I had done it to Cali. I had done this to myself.

Not wanting to leave him, I fell asleep in his arms. When I woke up in the morning, I was back in bed. Cali still wasn't there.

"I might have made a mistake," I admitted to Dillon as the realization hit me.

"Hil? What's going on?"

"There's something I haven't told you."

"What's that?" Dillon said, as if holding his breath.

"Someone put a bomb in my trunk," I said hesitantly.

"What!" he shouted in reply.

"Don't freak out."

"Don't freak out? Someone put a bomb in your trunk and you're telling me not to freak out? What would have happened if it exploded?"

I didn't respond.

"Hil?" he asked with horror in his voice.

"I'm fine. Cali and I are both fine."

"Hil, are you telling me the bomb exploded?"

"A little bit."

He was silent. I expected him to yell at me. Instead, all I heard were tears.

"I need to tell Remy where you are."

"I'm begging you, Dillon. Please don't. This is why I didn't tell you. I knew you would overreact."

"Hil, I could have lost you for the second time. I don't know what I would do if something happened to you and I could have done something to stop it."

"Cali is keeping me safe. In fact, he's keeping me too safe."

"There is no keeping you too safe, Hil."

"I think there is. I know everyone in my life is doing everything they can to stop bad things from happening to me. But it all might be too much."

"Hil, someone has tried to kill you twice."

"I know. And you're right. And before that, I had to worry about a rival family kidnapping me and using me against my father. And before that, I had to worry about being shot at because my father was encroaching on another family's territory.

"Each time it's for a very good reason. Everyone's trying to do everything they can to keep me safe. But, from where I'm standing, it just feels like the walls are closing in. This is no way to live. This was what I ran away from, and now it's followed me here."

"I'm so sorry, Hil. You shouldn't have to deal with this. Maybe it's selfish, but I just don't know what I would do without you."

"And I don't know what I would do without you. So, I understand. But, still…"

"It sucks," he said, finishing my thought.

"It sucks," I confirmed.

"I'm so sorry you have to go through this," he said with genuine empathy.

It took too much out of me to thank him, so I didn't. Instead, I brought the call to an end and laid in bed wondering how I would make it through another day. Again, resolving not to let it get to me, I got out of bed and checked in on Dr. Sonya.

"Good morning!" I said as cheerfully as I could.

"Good morning!" she said with as much energy back.

Maybe that was why I liked Dr. Sonya so much. Although we were from different worlds, we took the same approach to life. In spite of being stuck in bed, she was still quick with a smile. I understood that. Life was only bad when you let it get to you. If you focused on the good stuff, it was easier to smile.

I had to remember that. I had to focus on all the things I was grateful for. A few weeks ago, I was trapped in our penthouse with only one friend in the world. I had never been kissed, and the only person I'd ever seen naked was my brother. Now I had someone who loved me, strangers who looked out for me, and the view from my prison was the most beautiful view I could imagine. That counted as a win.

"You don't have to help me to the bathroom. I already went. It took a while to get there, but I started early," Dr. Sonya said joyfully.

"You didn't have to do that. I could have helped you. Did I wait too long to check in on you?"

"Don't be ridiculous. You've been fantastic. But I'm going to need to start to do some of these things by myself. There are plenty of things I've been slacking off with. They need to get done."

"If you let me know what they are, I can help you with them," I volunteered cheerfully.

She waved me off.

"They're just little things. I'm sure you know how it goes. Sometimes things just need a personal touch," she said with a smile.

"Of course," I said, hiding my disappointment that she didn't want my help.

Leaving her to make breakfast, I headed downstairs. Not seeing Cali, I hoped he had headed to campus for a class. It would have been the first time all week. But seeing his truck through the kitchen window, a wave of sadness overtook me.

I didn't know when but I knew that all of this would soon become too much to bare. I could feel myself starting to crack. I needed to get out of here. I needed to clear my head.

Without thinking, I grabbed the keys to my truck and headed to the door. Swinging it open and stepping onto the porch, I was startled.

"Where are you going?" Cali asked from the rocking chair on the other side of the bay window.

"Jesus! You scared me."

"I'm sorry," he said genuinely. "Where are you going?"

"I'm going to the grocery store," I told him continuing to the stairs.

"Stop!"

I froze.

"Tell me what you need. I'll go get it."

I thought about that. What did I need? The only thing I needed was to get away.

"Don't worry about it. I'll get it."

In a second, he proved to me that he was the football player I knew he was. In the blink of an eye, he was standing in front of me.

"Out of my way," I told him.

"I can't let you do that," he said with humility.

"You can't stop me. I'm going to the grocery store."

"And what happens if you go to the grocery store and out of nowhere someone kills you?"

"Cali, you're being ridiculous."

"I'm being ridiculous? Someone tried to run you off the road and then tried to kill you with a bomb!" he yelled. "How is me trying to keep you alive being ridiculous?"

"Cali, I'm living in a prison. This is why I left home. And now you're acting exactly like my father," I shouted, hoping he would understand.

His face hardened.

"You wanna go home. Is that it? You wanna leave? If you want, I'll drive you back. But I'm not letting you out of my sight until you're there. You might hate me, but at least you'll be alive," he told me, saying the cruelest thing he could have said.

I stared at him unsure what to do. Was this the end of us? It felt like it. What could I do now?

Chapter 14

Cali

Staring into the eyes of the man I loved, I was sure I was about to lose him. I was willing to live with it. Even if I couldn't be the man he needed me to be, I was going to keep him alive to find someone else. It would break my heart to see him go, but I couldn't stand it if something happened to him. I couldn't.

Looking up at me determining our fate, Hil's hot body melted. Defeated, he turned around and disappeared into the house. I watched him go. Even if he hadn't gone to collect his stuff, it felt as though I had lost him.

What did that change? Nothing. It was still my duty to keep him alive, and I would stop at nothing to make sure that happened.

Standing there dumbstruck, the only thing that brought me out of it was a familiar voice.

"What's going on, Cali?" my eldest brother asked me.

His large hand gripped my shoulder. Never having had a father, the feeling felt weird.

"I think I might have just lost him," I told Claude, terrified that it was true.

"No, I mean what's going on up here," he said, stepping in front of me and tapping on my forehead. "You know that this isn't right, correct? We'll all stay out here for as long as you need us to. We have your back. But it feels like there's something else going on. What is it?"

"I couldn't take it if something happened to him. I mean, I really couldn't take it," I told him with tears forming in my eyes.

I wasn't an emotional guy. Things didn't get to me. I made sure of it. But as I imagined losing him in all of the ways I could have, the feeling threatened to tear me apart. I could barely stand it.

"Who did you lose?" Claude asked me, cutting to the quick.

At first, I didn't know what he was talking about. I thought I was just trying to keep the boy I loved safe. And then it hit me. When the image filled my mind, I couldn't let it go.

"I lost Tim," I said in a whisper, overcome with emotion. "One day he seemed perfectly fine, and the next thing I know, my mother was telling me that he was being taken to a hospital out of state. I never saw him again. He was a guy I loved, and he had died. I didn't even get to say goodbye," I told my brother with tears rolling down my cheeks. "I can't lose Hil too. I can't lose him like I did Tim."

Claude wrapped his arms around me and held me tight. I couldn't control myself. Everything inside of me came pouring out. Hil had been right; I was imprisoning him. It wasn't an act of love. It was desperation.

He couldn't live like this. I couldn't either. I needed to free him. Or at least let him be free.

Leaving Claude, I wandered back to the porch and returned to my rocking chair. I thought about everything; Hil, Tim, the surgery I had yet to tell my mother she needed. How many mistakes had I made?

I should have told Tim how I felt about him before it was too late. Now that we had the money for her surgery, I needed to prepare her and set that all in motion. And I had to do the hardest thing I could imagine. I had to let Hil go.

He was right. He was living like a prisoner. This was the way to keep him alive, but this wasn't living. He deserved so much more than this. Maybe it was best for him to disappear again like he had from his family. Perhaps once he was gone and my mother could handle everything on her own, I could join him.

Whatever he did, it had to be his choice. He hadn't chosen the cage I had locked him in. And I had only done it because of my fear that I would lose him like I lost the only other guy I loved.

I couldn't keep doing this to him. Even if it meant losing him, I had to let him live. I just needed to make sure he knew how I felt about him before anything happened.

Abandoning my post on the porch, I went inside in search of Hil. He was in the kitchen making breakfast. Even with his back to me, I could tell he was crying. I had done this to him. My heart wrenched knowing that I had.

"Can I help you with anything?" I asked, standing in the doorway.

"Do I have any choice about it?" he spit, wounding me.

"I'll go," I told him, turning away.

"No," he said, stopping what he was doing to brace himself on the counter. "Cali, I'm mad at you," he said, not looking at me.

"I know. I'm sorry. I truly am."

"I know you are," he said, turning to face me with tear-stained cheeks. "And that's what makes it so frustrating. I know you're just trying to help me. Everyone's just trying to help me. But I'm not helpless. Can't anyone see that?"

"No one thinks you're helpless," I said, needing to comfort him. Holding his narrow forearms in my hand, I kissed his palms. "And, you're right. I wasn't giving you the respect you deserved. You're strong and capable. I'm sorry."

Accepting my apology, he freed his arms and placed his hands on my chest stepping closer to me.

"If you think I'm so capable, then why aren't you trusting me to defend myself?"

I held his shoulders, needing to touch him.

"You're right. I should have been," I conceded.

"No, I'm serious. Why was it that the first thing you did was to lock me up like I was a broken bird? I need to know. If you think I'm weak, you have to tell me. It's the only way I'll get stronger."

"That's not it," I assured him.

"But it has to be. What other explanation is there?"

I lowered my head as echoes of the past deafened me.

"You aren't the first guy I loved," I said almost at a whisper.

"What?"

"I said, when I was a kid there was another boy I loved."

Lifting my gaze from the floor, I found his eyes. I couldn't tell if it was hurt, surprise, or a mixture of every emotion that was staring back at me.

"Who was it?"

"He was my best friend."

"Have I met him?"

"He died."

Heartbreak reflected on Hil's face.

"I'm so sorry."

"It was my fault," I admitted for the first time saying it aloud.

"What? How?"

"I broke his heart."

Tears returned to Hil's eyes. "Tell me."

I gathered my strength. Taking a deep breath, I looked him in the eyes.

"From the first time he sat next to me at lunch, I knew there was something different about him. I never said anything about it. But I could feel it. It excited me. I wasn't sure why.

"As time went on, I started to figure it out. He would look at me, and when he did, my body would tingle. I knew what his staring meant. He liked me in a way that boys weren't supposed to. It was embarrassing, but mostly because I liked him that way too.

"The feeling was uncontrollable. I couldn't stop thinking about him. When I was with him, nothing else in the world mattered.

"I was willing to continue on this way, but eventually, Tim was not. The last time I saw him was one day when we went to our favorite creek to fish. Once we got there, he looked at me with light in his eyes. He told me he wanted to take a dip. When I agreed, he told me we should do it naked.

"As close as we were, we had never done that. I had fantasized about a lot of things with Tim by that point, so I wasn't sure what I should do. Eventually, I gave in to what we both wanted, and he didn't hide how excited he was at what we were doing.

"In spite of that, we floated close to each other. Neither of us said a word. And when we were practically on top of each other and he caught me staring at his excitement through the clear water, he leaned forward and kissed me.

"As much as I wanted it, what he did made me panic. I backed away and scrambled out. He tried to apologize as I got dressed but I wouldn't hear it. It wasn't that he wasn't kind and beautiful and the best friend that I had ever had. It was that I wasn't ready to accept who I was.

"When he tried to call me later, I ignored the call. I did the same thing when he tried to talk to me at school. And when it felt like everyone at lunch knew what we had done, I did something that I could never take back.

"There were a group of guys on the football team who I barely knew. They all sat at the same table and I knew that they could be jerks.

"Needing to prove how much of a man I was, I walked over to them and told them what Tim had done. There was no reason for it. They hadn't asked. But I outed my best friend for feeling the desire I also felt and they began making fun of him for it.

"I felt awful. I knew that I had done the worst thing anyone could do to someone they loved. And before I could ask for his forgiveness, his mother took him out of school. He had a condition that he hadn't shared with me, and the sadness he felt by my betrayal had lowered his immune system. He died from it.

"Maybe I hadn't pulled a trigger or hit him with a car, but it was my betrayal that had killed him. I'm sure of it. So now there's no way I'm not going to do everything I can to protect the man I love."

Hil stared at me with pain in his eyes. He didn't say word. Instead, he wrapped his arms around my waist and laid his cheek on my chest. I understood. There was nothing to say. My crime was undeniable. What I had done was unforgivable. I could never forgive myself.

"Thank you for telling me that," Hil said kindly.

After holding me for what felt like a long time, he pulled away.

"Would you like to help me with breakfast?" he asked, not bringing up the topic again.

The two of us made breakfast without saying a word. When it was done, he carried a tray up to Mama, and I set the table for our guests. Then the two of us sat in the kitchen and ate our breakfast alone.

When I reached across the table and took his hand, he didn't resist. I was grateful for that. He had such small, delicate hands. As soft as they were, I also felt their strength. I didn't deserve him. I knew that. But as long as I had him, I would do everything I could to make him happy.

That night as we lay in bed, I stared at him again considering how lucky I was. Facing him with our lips only inches apart, I leaned forward and kissed him. He barely kissed me back.

Needing more, I caressed his soft cheek with the back of my fingers. I could feel him relax. He was going to let me do anything I wanted to him. But all I wanted was to please him. So, slipping my hand underneath his shirt, I gently rubbed his back. And when his gentle movements melted into the subtle pushes from my fingertips, I sat up, rolled him onto his stomach, and removed his shirt.

I knew how to use my hands to please a man. Massage was the one form of physical touch that football players allowed. As I wrapped my large hands around Hil's narrow back, I engulfed him. His body was everything I ever wanted in a guy. Being allowed to express my affection for the boy I loved was the most erotic feeling of my life.

Applying more pressure, Hil's small body disappeared into the soft mattress. Rubbing his neck and shoulders, he moaned. I would have kept doing it all night if he hadn't begun lifting his hips. I was sitting on them. Initially I thought he wanted me to get off.

But the deeper I would push my fingers, the harder his hips would press. My baby was telling me what he wanted. I wanted to give it to him. Sliding my fingertips down the lean lines of his body, I got to his underwear and stopped. Shifting onto his legs, he lifted his hips again. Fulfilling his request, I took off his underwear.

Wanting nothing more than to please him, I massaged his ass and then lowered my chin between his cheeks. The touch of my tongue on his hole was electric. Grabbing the sheets, his body tensed. Teasing his rippled skin with the tip of my tongue, he struggled to breathe. And when I buried my face into his ass, his back curled in unbridled pleasure.

Pushing and taunting, I made Hil's asshole mine. His toes danced. His body wiggled.

Reducing him to a writhing mass, I wondered if I had relaxed him enough. Releasing him, his body collapsed. He was nothing more than a slab of meat on the mattress.

Rubbing my hard cock seeing what I had done, I couldn't fight how much I wanted him. And when my yearning became too much, I lowered my shorts and returned my hips to his ass.

The feeling of his tight hole fighting against my cock was everything I ever dreamed about. Lubing up and pushing harder, he opened up and welcomed me in. Buried inside of him, it felt like home.

Lying on top of him with our fingers intertwined and my body position mirroring his, I pulled back my hips and gently fucked. Withdrawing and thrusting, the two of us were one.

Shifting the top of my feet onto his soles, I held his hands and rode him harder. His groans were my siren song. The louder they got, the more he possessed me. I was a puppet. He pulled my strings. And when he pushed me off of him and climbed on top of me instead, I watched with pleasure as Hil took what he wanted.

My baby was a wild man. As big as I was, he rode me. Leaning forward with his palms on my chest, he hooked his feet between my thighs and galloped. When I couldn't take anymore and threatened to blow, I sat up, wrapped an arm around him, and allowed him to brace himself with his arms around my neck.

With my cock still deep inside of him, I lifted him as he bounced. This was when he leaned forward and kissed me. Cradling my head and with his tongue deep in my throat, I felt the pulse of orgasm rise and his breathing increase.

Still clutching my head, he bit my lip as our orgasms approached. I thought he would tear it off. He didn't. But throwing his head back, he came all over me. Spraying me with his cum, I filled him with mine.

I was going to do anything I had to do to keep this. Hil was the love of my life, and anything I had to sacrifice to have him, I would.

As soon as either of us could breathe again, Hil returned to our kiss. Gentler this time, he explored my lips. I wasn't sure if he had broken skin, but I could feel the tingle.

Shifting from there, his lips touched my cheekbones and the tip of my nose. Holding me as he did, I did nothing about it. He had me wrapped around his little finger whether he knew it or not. I was his and he was mine. And I couldn't fight the power he had over me if I tried.

The next morning when I woke up, I did what I hadn't in a while, I stayed in bed staring at the man I loved. Even as he slept, he was beautiful. He needed to be with someone who treated him how he deserved to be treated. I was going to be that man. It would start today. I had already waited too long.

When he opened his eyes, he caught me looking at him.

"Were you watching me sleep?" he asked with a chuckle.

"Are you okay with that? Because I watch you sleep a lot."

"It's not like I don't do the same thing to you," he said with the cutest stretch I had ever seen.

As we stared into each other's eyes, I gathered the courage to say what I had to say.

"Did you need to pick something up from the grocery store? I remember you mentioning something about that yesterday."

He perked up.

"Yeah. I don't remember what it was, but I would like to go."

"Would you mind if I went with you?"

He smiled and cuddled up against my chest.

"As long as you don't mind me hanging all over you when were there."

I wrapped my arm around him, pulling him to me.

"I guess it's something I will have to put up with."

"I guess you will," he said, warming my heart.

Lying in bed as long as we could, I held on to him trying to memorize every bend of his body.

"I should go," he told me when my mother's bell rang.

"I'm not sure what I would do without you," I admitted revealing the deepest part of my heart.

"If I have anything to say about it, you'll never have to know," he said with a smile.

Watching his naked body as he left the bed and got dressed, I was reminded of how lucky I was. He really was the most incredible guy I'd ever met.

I was going to be the type of guy he needed. I would sacrifice anything I had to to give him everything he could dream of. I was all in for him. And there was nothing I wanted more then to see him happy.

Getting dressed, I decided to give him a break and make the breakfast. I had to admit that he had quickly developed a knack for it. Experimenting with new ingredients, his waffles were better than mine had ever been.

Hoping he wouldn't be disappointed, I quickly threw together the batter. By the time he joined me in the kitchen, the steam was already rising from the waffle maker.

"I added the berries to the batter. I don't know how it will taste. But I had to step up my game considering the wiz you've become in the kitchen," I said with a smile.

"It's not a competition. It can't be with me winning so much," he joked teasingly.

It was almost enough to ruffle my competitive feathers. What was a friendly competition between friends, right?

With everyone else fed and it being just the two of us, I asked him if I could feed him the waffles. He said I could. There was something about it that made me feel good.

I gave him a bite and then I took a bite. And every so often I would lean over and give him a kiss. When there was nothing left on our plates and we were both full, we got ready for the day.

"So, are we still heading to the grocery store?" he asked me with vulnerability in his eyes.

"Of course. After cooking I can see how embarrassingly short we are on supplies," I said with a smile.

It wasn't true. But if he needed me to play along to give us an excuse, I was more than happy to.

Dressed and ready to go, I grabbed my keys offering to drive. I wasn't going to look around every tree as we did it either. I was going to be present and to pay attention to him. He was the most important thing in my life. I was going to show him that.

Focusing on Hil was easier than I thought it would be. Stepping into Glen's, we were holding hands. It felt good showing the world that he was mine.

"Good morning!" Glen said as we entered.

"Morning," each of us said with a smile.

Browsing the aisles, I wondered if every day of our lives could be like this. I would pick up things and show it to him. He would shake his head, encouraging me to put it back.

"Are you sure that we don't need pickled herrings? You don't know waffles until you've put pickled herrings on them," I hold him.

"I'm going to pray that you're joking," he said, staring at me horrified.

"Do you seriously think that I would put pickled herrings on waffles?"

"I don't know. I'm in the South. Don't you all put pickled herrings on everything?"

"Do you even know what pickled herrings are?"

"Sure. It's herrings that have been pickled," he said, as if trying to get away with something.

"Right. Just like how baseball is a ball with a base inside of it," I teased.

"Oh yeah? Then you tell me what pickled herrings are, smart guy."

I stared at him.

"Well, that's easy."

I stared at him again. "Glen, would you like to inform this city boy on what pickled herrings are?"

"I would be delighted to, Glen said, approaching us. "If you take a look at this," Glen said, crouching to retrieve something from the shelf. "Now, where is it?"

Hil tapped me on my shoulder telling me he would be right back.

"Oh, here it is. This here is a dill pickle. It's like that because of the vinegar that's added to water when the pickle is soaked. If you take the same process and add it to a fish, like hearing, it changes the flavors and…" Glen looked around. "Where did Hil go? Should I wait for him before I continue?"

I turned around expecting Hil to be behind me. He wasn't.

"Hil?" I said, scanning the room.

He couldn't have gone far. He was behind me just a second ago.

"Hil?" I said, getting worried when he didn't respond. "Hil!"

Terror washed through me. Racing down the aisles, I checked every floor and corner. It was then that I heard him scream.

"Hil!" I said rushing to the door.

It was in time to see a brutal looking man covered from his neck to his wrist in tattoos. In one hand he held a knife. In the other, Hil.

"Hey!" I shouted hoping the windows would shatter as I did.

That didn't stop him. It barely slowed him down. Looking back at me, he opened his car door and shoved Hil in. Running towards them, I wasn't quick enough to get there before he slipped in the driver side, started the car, and pull off.

It was a C-Class Mercedes. It matched the description of what Hil had said had been stalking him. This was the man who had tried to kill Hil twice. He had gotten him. I had taken my eyes off of him for a second and it had been enough.

"No!" I screamed as the guy drove away.

Rushing to my truck, I got in and sped off after them. It took only a moment to realize what the guy's knife was for. One of my tires were flat. I had no chance of keeping up with them. Speeding out of town at the pace that they were, they would be gone before anyone could do anything about it.

My worst nightmare was coming true. I was losing Hil, and it was all my fault. I wouldn't be able to catch him, and I wouldn't be able to forgive myself.

Falling further and further behind the accelerating car, my will to go on escaped me. I drove until I couldn't drive anymore. But with every passing second, my love disappeared into the distance.

I had lost Hil. What was I going to do now?

Chapter 15

Hil

I screamed as the man I loved receded into the landscape. I don't know if it was out of rage or fear. And when I saw the steely look in the man who was taking me from him, I was ready to do to him what I was told that my father did to others.

"You had no right to do this. No right! Take me back right now," I demanded ready to reach over and strangle him.

"You will do what I tell you to do," he said menacingly.

"You don't scare me. Maybe you did once. But not anymore," I said, not backing down an inch.

For a moment, the driver looked like he would hit me. But he didn't. Instead, his eyes softened. He ceased to be my father's enforcer and again became my brother.

"Hil, I have to take you back."

"You don't have to do anything. Neither of us do. I thought we did. That was a lie that we were fed from when we were old enough to walk. But I left all this behind. You can too."

Remy didn't speak. I couldn't tell if he refused to accept what I was saying or if he didn't believe it.

He and I had lived different lives growing up. He was the son who no one dared to mess with. And with good reason.

One of the few times my father had allowed me to go to a party, I had gone thinking I would have a good time. Alone with the other kids, one of the other boys had called me a faggot and had started making fun of me. Remy found out and nearly beat the boy to death.

For a long time, I wondered if the reason I wasn't allowed out was because my brother was too protective. I couldn't hide who I was and the kids around me couldn't stand it. So there was no stopping Remy from doing what he would do to protect me. Was I not allowed to go out because he would have ended up in jail?

That didn't stop me from hating my brother as much as I loved him. Now here he was taking me from the first guy who had made me feel like I was worth something. I was pretty sure I hated him again.

"I will never forgive you for this," I told him realizing it was true.

"Hate me all you want. You're gonna do it anyway," he said with a chill in his eyes.

"You don't know what you're stealing me from, Remy. If you did, you wouldn't be doing this."

"Oh yeah? Then tell me."

"You wouldn't understand."

"Why? Because I have no heart? That's always what you've thought about me, isn't it? That I am a mindless thug, one incapable of feelings?"

"You know me so well," I said, hoping it would hurt him as much as he was hurting me.

"Do you think I like doing this to you? Is that why you think I'm here?"

"No. I'm sure you have some good excuse why you're following father's insane orders. Would you have killed Cali if he had tried to stop you?"

"Hil, I've never killed anyone."

"Yeah, right. You and father, you're both priests," I said snidely.

Remy swallowed. I had found his nerve. I was considering how much to poke it when something in him changed.

"I'm not the animal you think I am, brother."

"And I'm not the helpless gay boy that you think I am," I insisted.

"I've never thought you were helpless. Never! Not once!"

"Then why do you act like it every chance you get?"

"Because one of us needs to live in the real world. We don't get to have lives like other people do.

We're Lyons. They try to take us down at every turn. We have to be hard to stay alive.

"For some reason, you don't seem to get that. Or maybe you're incapable of mustering that type of resolve. But we do what we need to to survive. One day you'll learn that. The rest of us just need to keep you breathing until you do."

I didn't say anything to him after that. It was partly because I was too busy hating him and partly because I knew what he said was true.

My father once said that 'You don't raise a lion on a beach when they need to survive in a jungle.' Our crazy life was a jungle, yet I refused to act like it. I refused to fight. I refuse to deceive. I refuse to look another man in the eyes and then punch him in the face.

That wasn't me. I wanted no part of it. Yet, that was the life I was born into. Maybe Remy and my father were right. Maybe I was never meant to survive.

The car was quiet as Remy drove us back to New York. More than anything else, I thought about how he had found me. Had Dillon told him where I was? I couldn't blame him if he did. Perhaps I would betray him too if it meant saving his life.

Did I hate him as much as I did Remy for taking me? I wasn't sure. All I knew was that my brother was returning me to prison.

For a while, I had escaped and lived my dream. But it was time to face what I had run from. It was time to face why I had ran.

After a night which included sleeping in the car, we re-entered the busy city streets of downtown Manhattan. Entering the building I no longer considered home, we parked. Following my brother to the elevator, we took it to the top floor. Using his key, the door opened spilling us out onto the foyer.

"Mother? Father? I'm home. I found him," Remy said, leaving me to retire to his room.

Remy always did the dirty work. He never cared to see the result.

"Hil?" my mother said, appearing in the doorway at the end of the hall. "Oh my God, Hil! Where have you been?" she said, running and throwing her arms around me.

"I was away having a life, Mother. That's where I was. I'd found someone who loved me and a world where I could fit in. Why did you all bring me back here?"

"It was your father. He needs to see you," she told me, still holding me tightly. "And, you need to see him."

"I don't want to," I confessed, feeling ashamed.

"I know you don't. But you have to. No matter what else he has done, he's still your father. If you let this time slip away, you'll regret it. I'm telling you as a person filled with regrets," my mother said, letting me go, yet staring me in the eyes.

If there was anyone who I took after in the family, it was her. Her loosely curly hair was speckled with gray. Her fair skin, freckled.

In spite of being an age past what most men chased after, everyone still stared at her. It was a point of pride for my father. It made him feel like a big man.

But what I admired most about my mother was her kindness. She was able to love a man who most people couldn't. Past that, she was able to love me. Not even I was capable of doing that.

"See him," she said holding my hand in hers.

"Mother…"

"Please, for me. Talk to your father," she requested in the way that I could never resist.

Knowing that there was no way I could escape it, I went to the place I knew he would be. Entering what used to be his office, I looked across the room and saw him. He was in worse shape than I could have imagined.

It wasn't one of his rivals who was bringing him down, it was something none of us could have imagined. One day while watching a football game, he had a stroke. That would have been nothing if he hadn't then had another and still another.

When he could no longer stop us from doing what we had to, we took him to the doctor. It turned out that he had cancer. That was what was causing the strokes. He wasn't given long to live.

Soon, the man I grew up thinking was indestructible was going to be gone. That was what had caused me to run. I needed to prove to him that I was going to be fine without him. I needed to show him that I was capable of more than he thought I was.

"Hil, is that you?" he asked too weak to hide his French accent.

"Yes, Father. I'm here."

"I missed you, son. Where have you been?" he asked showing the side of him that I had rarely seen.

"I was…"

How did I explain to him what I was doing? The answer was that I was everything. I was loving. I was living, I was experiencing things I thought I never would.

"I was forging a new life for myself. One where you wouldn't have to worry about me."

"That's not possible. I will always worry about you," he said with a fragile smile.

"But, Father, you always had that wrong. I'm capable of taking care of myself," I insisted.

He dismissed me with a shake of his head.

"These are dangerous times, Hil. Word has gotten out that I'm sick. Families are doing everything they can to take over our territory. You are not safe. Lying here, I cannot protect you."

I stared at the withering man in front of me understanding something I hadn't before. That was why someone had tried to run me off the road. Our family was in a middle of a war. They were doing what my father once had; they had gone for blood once they smelled weakness.

As long as we had something they wanted, no one would leave our family alone. I really was trapped here. There was nowhere I could go and be safe.

"Do you have any regrets, Father?" I asked him, considering my own.

He thought for a moment and then smiled.

"Not a one. We have a short time on this planet. You seize what you can while you can. I had your mother and I had my two beautiful kids. With that I created an empire and soon I'm going to pass it along to you two. What is there to regret in that?" my father said before becoming too weak to speak.

Leaving him to rest, I crossed the penthouse to my room. It was across the hall from my brother's. From outside, I could hear the soprano from his favorite aria. He once told me it was his way of escaping.

If there was one thing I was jealous of him for, it was that he found a way to not be here even when he was. There were so many things about our two lives that were unfair. That had to be the most.

About to enter my room, I stopped. I knew that once I passed the doorway, it was official, I was back.

Again, I was trapped. The weight of it prevented me from moving forward. With a mixture of sadness and anger, I spun towards my brother's bedroom door and burst in.

Startled, Remy instinctually reached under his desk and pulled out a gun. Seeing it didn't phase me. I was pissed and there was nothing he was going to do to scare me off.

Seeing me, Remy relaxed.

"Jesus, Hil. I almost shot you. Are you insane? Why would you burst in like that?"

"Why did you do it? Why did you take me from the only place I've ever been happy? How could you do that to me?" I asked on the brink of tears.

Calmly, Remy returned his gun to its hiding spot and faced his computer screen.

"Father wanted to see you."

"And he gets whatever he wants? Is that it? None of us gets a say on our own lives?"

Remy looked at me confused.

"You say that like you're new here."

"This is unfair, Remy. I didn't ask for any of this. You might like being a part of father's crazy world, but where do I fit into it? I can't live like this. You should have left me where I was. Whatever happened to me there, at least it would have been from my own choices."

Remy's eyes darted to me.

"What do you mean, 'whatever happened to you there?' What happened to you there?"

I froze as Dr. Sonya's accident and the bomb flashed to mind. Remy didn't know. So, he had retrieved me simply because father had told him to. If Dillon had told him where I was, wouldn't he have also mentioned what had happened to me?

"What aren't you telling me? You know I've always been able to tell when you're lying. You're not good at it. Don't start now."

I stared at him starting to panic. What would he do if he knew that there was already someone after me? The bars around my cage would lock even tighter. This conversation was a mistake.

"Nothing happened to me there," I told him before turning to go.

"You're lying. I told you, you're not good at it."

"Leave me alone," I told him, exiting his room and entering mine.

Never being able to let anything go, Remy followed me. Behind my closed door, I locked it and stepped back.

"Hil?" Remy said, finding the door locked. "Are you serious? Open the door."

"This is my room. Stay out of it. Leave me alone," I said feeling a cold sweat.

"Don't make me do this, Hil," he said calmly.

"Leave me alone!" I shouted, praying that he would.

When silence followed, I held my breath. It wasn't until I exhaled that my door burst open and my intimidating brother entered.

"Doesn't feel so good, right?" he said, justifying what he had done.

"If you had locked your door, I would have respected it."

"You mean for the first time?" Remy retorted with a smirk.

He wasn't wrong. No one in this house respected locked doors. The only thing that ever kept us out is the fear of what we would find when we entered.

For example, both Remy and I learned early that when my parents were in their bedroom, we did not want to see what was going on. Those were images that no amount of alcohol would ever erase.

Walking in on Remy while he was enjoying porn was another story. Sure, it was nothing that I wanted to see. But our parents, who couldn't keep their hands off of each other, had created an environment where sexuality wasn't something to be afraid of. So, if I wanted to get back at Remy for being an asshole big brother, I would wait until everything got really quiet in his room and then pick the lock and throw open the door.

What can I say? I spent my entire life locked in this penthouse. I got bored. Watching a teenaged Remy rush to close this computer while pulling up his pants was entertaining.

"I told you to leave," I insisted, not backing down.

"And I told you to tell me what happened there. Would you prefer that I told father that there's something going on? How do you think he would respond to that?"

"You would rat me out to father? Aren't you gangster type supposed to have a code?" I said trying to think of anything I could to get him to drop it.

"We do have a code. It's called, keep your family alive even when they're trying to get themselves killed. You should try it sometime. Maybe start with yourself," Remy said, slowly breaking down my defenses.

When I continued to refuse to answer, he took a different approach. Instead of being the demanding, asshole brother, he crossed to my desk chair, turned it towards me, and sat leaning forward with his fingers intertwined.

"Hil, if you tell me what's going on, I promise not to tell father. You know you can trust me, right?"

"Considering you just took me from my only chance at happiness, I think trust might be the wrong word. Loathe? Hate?"

Remy's lips tightened in frustration.

"I've never broken my word to you. And it's been a long time since I've lied. I found you because father is dying. We don't know how much longer he has left and he wanted to say bye to his son.

"I figured, once you knew, you would want to see him too. I also knew that father didn't want to tell you that. He doesn't like to look weak. Not even to his own kids.

"So I needed you here, I couldn't tell you why, and I didn't want to waste the little time father has left negotiating. There you have it. Right or wrong, that's what went down. Now, what is it that you're not telling me?"

I considered everything Remy had said. It was true. He had always been very straight with me. In a weird way, he was the one I trusted the most. He had always protected me and he had always been honest, even when I didn't what to hear the truth.

What had upset me was that he knew how unhappy I was. I had thought that even if our father had asked him to find me, he wouldn't. I was mad because his retrieving me felt like a betrayal. But listening to his explanation, maybe it wasn't.

"Father is dying?" I asked as it sunk in. "How long do the doctors say that he has?"

"It could be days; it could be a few weeks. Anytime you talk to him, it could be the last thing you ever say to him. That's why I brought you home. I couldn't let him die without giving you the chance to say goodbye."

Remy's words were a punch in the gut. It took everything in me not to cry. I had a lot of mixed feelings about my father, but I loved him. He wasn't a good person. He wasn't a trusted businessman. But he did love us, and he told us every chance he got.

"What happens to us when he's gone?" I asked, starting to spiral.

"I have come up with a plan. There's a way that we can get out of all this. We won't have to worry about looking over our shoulders everywhere we go. There's a way we can go legitimate.

"But if something happened to you that I need to know about and you don't tell me, it could derail everything. We'll all be stuck in this world for the rest of our lives. And some of our lives might be shorter than others," Remy said with empathetic conviction.

I stared at Remy considering what he had said. Could it be true? Was there a chance that we could escape this world? We certainly couldn't do it while my father was alive. For him, all of it was a game that he loved too much to quit. This was his reason to get up in the morning. As much as he loved us, we could never compete with it.

"How?" I asked praying that it was real.

"Are you asking me about my plan?"

"Yeah," I said hesitantly.

"It is all moving too fast to explain. But, trust me, I want out of this life as much as you do. But the only shot we have of getting out relies on you shutting down whatever it is you had going on and telling me what happened."

I didn't move in fear that it would prevent his dream from coming true. More so than guys or anything else, that was what I laid in bed fantasizing about. Remy knew this. Was he just telling me what I wanted to hear to get what he wanted? And what did he mean by me shutting down whatever I had going on?

Damn him, he knew me too well.

"If you're lying…" I said with building anger.

"I'm not. There is a plan. But it's going to take everyone in this family agreeing to it for it to work. So, tell me, what are you hiding?"

He had me. He had made the stakes too high.

"I think someone made two attempts on my life?"

"What!" Remy said flying into a rage.

"A few weeks ago, I let a friend drive the car I took and someone ran it off a mountain road."

"I can't believe this. How is the person who was driving your car?"

"They need surgery, but it seems they'll be all right."

"I'll make arrangements to take care of their bills."

"No need. I already have."

"Please tell me you didn't," Remy said, about to panic.

"Don't worry. I gave them cash. It was what I had on me from my trip. I'm pretty sure it'll cover everything."

"Okay," Remy said relaxing. "And the second attempt?"

"Well, like I said, because of the accident, the car ended up stuck on the side of a mountain. I needed the cash inside of it to pay for the surgery. But, when I opened the trunk, there was a bomb in it. It exploded."

Remy looked at me suspiciously.

"And was everyone all right?"

"Yeah. It seems like the person who put it there wasn't very good at make triggers," I joked.

Remy stared at me stone faced until he laughed.

"My brother, living every day thanks to the incompetence of others."

"You know what father says, always count on people to be idiots," I said with a smile.

"You should not be betting your life on it, Hil. You got lucky, twice. You're not a cat. You don't have that many lives. You're going to need to put an end to things with whoever that was chases us as we pulled off."

"I'm not going to do that, Remy," I informed him.

"You are. If there really was someone trying to kill you and they knew where you were and how to get to you, how safe do you think your friends are in that small town? You can't give your assassin a reason to think that you might be back. Hil, it's the safest thing for everyone involved, especially you," he said, trying to sound reasonable.

I couldn't count the number of times I had laid in bed wondering how much danger I had put Cali in. I knew that what I was doing was unfair to him. I couldn't deny it. But, how could I not be with a man like that? He loved me. I loved him. But, did loving him mean that I would have to let him go? It was too painful to think about.

"Is there anything else you're not telling me?" Remy asked while giving me an unwavering look.

"I found a guy who loved me. He was kind and thoughtful, and I fell in love with him," I said showing my brother my heart.

"Oh Hil, you can't believe that what you felt was love. How long were you gone? Did he even tell you his real name?"

I stared at Remy dumbstruck. The anger I felt prevented me from unpacking the craziness he said in so few words. There was no way I would be able to respond to any of it, so instead I said, "Have you ever been in love, Remy?"

Remy smiled.

"I have been in love many times. And then I got dressed and went home."

I stared at him. If there's one thing that Remy kept to himself, it was his love life. What I imagined was a string of one-night stands with beautiful women that would commit their life to him before either had the chance to get dressed. Like I said, I had seen my brother naked.

But past that, I didn't know much about him. Did he like them short? Tall? Was every woman in this bed exactly like our mother? Had he ever been in love?

"You have no idea what love is, do you?" I asked when it hit me.

"I know enough to make me want to protect you all these years," he said smugly.

"That's fair. But do you know what it feels like to be *in* love?" I asked him, knowing the answer. When he didn't respond, I said, "If you knew what that felt like, you wouldn't be asking me to do what you are to Cali."

"Then it's a good thing I don't, because that wouldn't change whether or not I'm right. You tell me, Hil, am I right? Is it safest for this guy that you never see him again?"

Every muscle in my chest clenched. I couldn't breathe. I was drowning. And the longer I considered Remy's question, the deeper into the abyss I fell.

"Can you give me some privacy, please," I said climbing onto my bed and looking away.

Remy exited the room without a word. Gently closing the door behind him, the silence became overwhelming.

I truly and sincerely loved Cali with all my might. Dillon had once said that when you know, you know. With Cali, I had no doubt.

If I walked away from him, I would never experience anything like what we had again. He had rescued me without even knowing it. He gave me a world after growing up without one.

I didn't need money or status. All I needed was a bed-and-breakfast in some small town with the guy who ran it and the family that surrounded him. I had hit a home run during my first time at bat.

How could I now walk away from it all? The thought of it threatened to reduce me to tears. But how could I go back to him knowing the risk I posed to his life? His mother had already been put into the hospital because of me. In the explosion, Cali might have died.

Remy was right. If I loved him, I had to let him go. I would think about him every day for the rest of my life, but I could never be with him.

Tears streamed down my face when I realized that my decision had been made. Retrieving my phone, I searched the internet for a bed-and-breakfast in Snow Tip Falls. When the number came up, I dialed it. The ringing was deafening; my soul laid bare.

Chapter 16

Cali

Thinking about how I had let him down, my world was coming apart. My thoughts whipped from how much I hated myself to how worried I was for him. How could I have done that? I had taken my eyes off of him and in the second I had he was gone.

This was my fault. I could never forgive myself for this. Even after the car had disappeared into the distance, I had continued to follow. I didn't stop until my truck couldn't drive anymore. I considered taking the time to replace the tire, but once it was off, I realized I had done more damage than I could have imagined.

Having to call my brothers to let them know what had happened, it wasn't long before someone was out to get me. Climbing into Claude's truck and driving until we hit the first turn off, it was there where he told me that we had to go home. We didn't have to stop looking, but we were going to have to come up with a new plan.

Sitting in the living room as everyone argued about what we should do next, I felt like I was going insane. I had lost him just like I had lost Tim. Again, it had been all my fault. I didn't deserve to be alive. I should have done more. But I didn't know what I could have done.

Deadlocked between calling the FBI and trying to figure out who his family was and contacting them, I walked around in a daze. Titus and Cage tried to comfort me. There was nothing they could say. I wasn't worthy of comfort. I didn't deserve to feel better. How could I have let him down so completely? There was no way I was going to be able to live knowing that.

As it approached evening the next day, I was approaching a decision. Although it wasn't what I or any of my brothers wanted, I decided not to call the FBI. It was the only thing I knew that Hil wanted. He was adamant about it. That meant that there was only one option. I was going to have to figure out who his family was and tell them.

The only problem was that Hil had been very tight-lipped about his life before meeting me. I knew he was from New York. He had once mentioned a brother. And there was something important about lions when it came to his family.

Did mafia families have crests? I knew nothing about them. Organized crime wasn't something you'd find in a town like Snow Tip Falls. Nor was it something that appeared on an Internet search. How had I not learned more about him? It felt like I knew exactly who he was. Yet, I didn't even know his last name.

A part of that was because I was a horrible person who didn't deserve him. The other part, though, was that he didn't seem interested in sharing. I wasn't the type to ask a lot of questions. So after he told me that his family was involved in organized crime, I stopped asking completely. What was I supposed to do now?

It was as I considered all the ways I could research New York's mafia families that I heard the phone ring. It was the business's phone connected to the landline in my mother's room. Before I could make a move to get it, the ringing stopped. And when I heard my mother's bell requesting that I assist her, I hurried in.

I might have failed Hil, but I wasn't going to continue to fail my mother. Rushing up the stairs, I entered her room. She was looking at me with frustration. Having placed the call on hold, she asked the question I had been avoiding answering.

"I've been patient. I figured that when the time came, you would tell me. I thought it had to do with your football team or something, so I wasn't going to pry. But now this," she said holding up the phone. "I need an explanation right now."

I stared at the phone confused.

"Who's that?"

"Hil," my mother said, filling my forehead with cold sweat.

Before my mother could object, I rushed to her and took the phone.

"Where are you?" I said in a panic.

"I am home," he replied with sadness.

"I don't understand. What happened?"

"The guy you saw taking me was my brother, Remy. He needed me home and he wasn't in the mood to debate about it."

"So he just took you? Are you alright?"

"I'm pissed off and furious, but physically I'm fine."

"I still don't understand. Why did he take you like that? When are you coming back?"

The silence between us drew out. When I heard him crying, I spoke up.

"Hil, when are you coming back?"

Sounding like he was gathering every ounce of courage he had, he said, "I'm not."

My chest felt like it was on fire.

"What do you mean you're not coming back?"

"I have already put you in enough danger. Your mother was in that accident because of me. You could have been killed by a bomb because of me. Previously, I could have fooled myself into believing that, somehow it wasn't my fault. But it was. I understand now. My brother explained it to me. I am not safe to be around.

And I love you too much to put you in danger," he said, breaking my heart.

"I don't care if being with you is risky. I'll take that risk. You're worth it, every second of it."

"You say that, and I believe you. But would you be willing to allow your mother to be hurt again?" he said, causing my eyes to bounce to the woman who was still recovering from her accident. "And what if the next time it's one of your brothers or an innocent bystander who didn't ask for any of this? How would you be able to live with yourself then? I know I couldn't. And that's the reason I won't be contacting you again."

The blood rushed out of my face having heard what he had said. I couldn't believe it. He was breaking up with me. I didn't want him to go. I would have done anything to be in his life. But a part of me knew that he was right. I would do anything and go anywhere to be with him. But, did that give me the right to put everyone I cared about in danger?

"I love you, Hil," I told him, struggling to stay upright.

Hil exploded into tears.

"I love you too, Cali."

"I can't let you go."

"Then, I will let you go. Bye, Cali. I will never stop thinking about you," he said before the line went dead.

I couldn't believe it. Hil was gone. All I could hear was a loud buzzing. I couldn't see what was in front of me. The only thing I could picture was what I had just lost.

"I'm so sorry," Mama said.

I looked at her. Tears were rolling down her cheeks. She had heard everything. I didn't know what I was supposed to say to her. So, instead of saying anything, I handed her the phone and walked out.

Once in the hallway, I continued walking. Descending the stairs, I headed for the front door.

"Cali, what happened? Where are you going?" Claude asked as I continued onto the porch.

Without saying a word, I walked down the driveway and onto the street. Still in a daze, I entered the woods. When I stopped walking I was in front of a creek. It was the one where Tim and I had skinny dipped all those years earlier.

Stripping off my clothes, I got in. It was cold. That was fine. And releasing the grip I held tightly for so long, the dam broke. I sobbed.

I don't know how long I was there. I know that it was longer than I needed to pull myself together. I could have stayed there forever. I might have if it wasn't for my mother. She needed me. I had to fix her dinner. I wasn't going to let her down.

She had also asked me not to let my education slip. I had. If nothing else, I could fix that. I just needed to show up. Wasn't that the case? Wasn't showing up half the battle?

Getting out and getting dressed, I walked back home. When I was there, I started making dinner. It wasn't anything special, but it was all I could manage.

"Would you like to talk?" my mother asked me as I set the tray down in front of her.

It wasn't that I was ignoring her. I was just tackling everything I could handle at the moment. Even shaking my head would have been too much. So instead, I looked at her. When she understood, I left to start cleaning up the mess I left behind.

The next morning, I drove to campus and attended class. I took notes. I participated in the discussion. And when the campus bell rang, I packed up my stuff and headed to the next one.

For the following days and the next two weeks, that was all I did. It was during that time that I told Mama everything that had gone on. I told her about Hil's family, why someone had run her off the road, and the surgery that she needed. She took everything well.

When she asked about the things we could do to get the money, I told her about Hil's gift. She wasn't sure how to respond. Mama had always raised me to have a respect for the law. It wasn't that knowing Hil's background had tarnished her view of him. She still loved him like a son. It was that she considered his family's money to be ill gotten gains.

"He wanted you to have it. He was very clear. He thought that something good had to come out of the things his family did. And I want you to take it. It would make me feel like I wasn't going through all this pain for nothing," I admitted to Mama, sharing more with her than I had since Tim died.

It took a long time for her to speak again. When she did, there was sadness in her eyes.

"There's a reason I've never told you about your father."

Having not expected this, my gaze flicked up at her.

"What is it?" I asked, having suddenly lost my breath.

"Your father wasn't on a good path," she admitted not being able to look me in the eyes.

I was desperate to know more.

"What do you mean?"

"When you told me about Hil, I had to wonder if the reason you had fallen for someone like him was because of who I had once fallen for."

She looked up at me offering a sad smile.

"There are times when you remind me so much of him. He was so determined. He could be so charismatic. But he was also secretive. He had a dark side.

"Obviously I wasn't the only one who had fallen for his charms. I had no idea about them—your brothers' mothers. That was as much of a surprise to me as it was when you found out about it. I guess I was embarrassed that I had been seduced so easily.

"He really was so handsome, though. That's where you get your good looks from. And you turned out to be the best thing that ever happened to me," she said with a smile.

"Who was he?" I asked, not wanting the conversation to end.

"A guy I met. Someone dark and dangerous. Someone who made me feel special."

"Is he anyone I know?"

"No. And I'm hoping he's someone you'll never know."

"What if I wanna know him?"

My mother didn't respond. Instead, she said,

"I've began to wonder if I've made the wrong decision with him. After he found out that I was pregnant with you, he did ask me to stay. I didn't want to raise you in that world, though. I didn't think you would make it past twenty. What chance does someone have growing up with a role model like that? I wanted you to be able to choose the direction of your life, not have them chosen for you.

"And I never second guessed that decision until you told me about Hil's family. Was there a path somewhere in there where you could have become Hil?

Could you have been happy? Could you have turned out all right?

"Who is to say? But one thing I do know is that Hil is not your father. There are some risks that, no matter the consequence, is worth taking. Sometimes you have to ask yourself, is he the right risk for you."

I stood stunned. In those few minutes I had learned more about myself and my mother than I had my entire life. I had given up Hil for her as much as anyone. In a roundabout way, had she told me that she had regretted her choice to leave my father? I wasn't sure. But what I was sure about was that she wanted me to be with the man I loved.

I had tried to live without him. But what I had been doing these past few weeks wasn't living. I was alive, but that was it. Was there another way?

What he had said was true. Being with him was a risk to everyone around me. But, what if the only one around me was him? Was I willing to give up everything to be with him? I still had three years left at school. I had my mother who would need help even after surgery. And I had my brothers who I was just starting to get to know.

But, Hil was my guy. I was sure of it. I didn't want him to go through everything he had to alone.

He hadn't asked to be born into the family he was. He didn't do anything to invite the danger that surrounded him. He needed me even more than my mother or my brothers did.

I needed to be there for him whether he asked me to or not. I loved that man. His pain was my pain. And I wasn't going to take no for an answer.

Deciding that nothing was going to stop me, I first considered how I was going to contact him. He had never given me his number. He didn't have to. We had been living together.

The only time we had spoken on the phone was when he called to break things off. It was on our landline. Did landlines work like cell phones? Could I get a list of every call that was made or received if I looked at the bill?

Knowing the day that he called, I signed into our account online and found it. I was stunned. I had the number he called me from. I could call him back. What was I going to say?

Calling him from a cell phone, I listened as it rang. When he saw my name, would he pick up? He had made it clear that he had wanted things to be over between us. But hadn't he also said that he loved me?

"Hello?" Hil's beautiful voice said, making my heart melt.

"Hil?"

"Cali, I don't know if you should be calling me," he said with an all too familiar sadness.

"I had to. I know what you said. I remember. But please, hear me out. Will you do that?"

For a moment, there was only silence.

"Yes," he eventually said, giving me a hint of hope.

This was it. This could be the last time I ever spoke to him, or it could be the beginning of the rest of our lives. I couldn't mess this up. What could I tell him that would change his mind? I didn't know. So, all that was left was to speak from the heart.

"You know I love you. You know I would do anything to protect you. So, that's not what I want to say. What I want to say is that I don't want you to be alone.

"On the days that you're sad and you need someone to hold your hand and just be there for you, I want to be the one. When you're feeling cranky for no good reason and you just need to be picked up, I want to be with you. During the times when you're thinking about how unfair life is and that you got put into positions that no one should have to go through, I wanna go through it with you.

"You don't deserve to go through this alone. Any of this. You are the most incredible guy I've ever met, and you deserve to be with someone who sees it and loves it and can't live without it.

"If it's not me, it should be someone else. I'm hoping it's me, though. Because the idea of sharing a life with you makes me happier than anything I can imagine.

"You are the star I sail towards. You are my reason to wake up. Will there be risks? Yes. But aren't there always?

"Relationships are nothing but risks. I could end up hurt. So could you. So could everyone around us. But that shouldn't stop us.

"We'll do everything we can to keep the ones we love safe. I could move there. We both could move somewhere else. But, whatever it takes, I need you. I love you. I want to be with you. And if you would consider being with me, it would make me the happiest guy alive.

"So, what do you say? Will you give us try?" I said for the first time, speaking entirely from my heart.

Every second that passed in silence was a century. I aged waiting for him to speak. When he did, I didn't know what he would say. So, when he said, "I could never live without you," I remembered how to breathe.

"I need to see you," I told him meaning it.

"I need to see you too," he said sounding as desperate as I was.

"But, how?"

"I've been thinking about this."

"You've been thinking about this?" I said with a smile.

"All I've done is think about you," he said melting my heart.

"What have you been thinking?"

He paused.

"I have a plan."

Chapter 17

Hil

I couldn't do it. I knew the best thing for everyone was if I forgot about Cali. I should have moved on and somehow pretended that the last few weeks with him hadn't happened. But I could barely breathe without him.

I tried to get out of bed. I truly did. It was like my arms didn't work. My legs couldn't move. Everything on me ached. I needed Cali.

But no one deserved to be hurt because of me. So, as I stared at the ceiling with uncontrollable tears rolling down the sides of my face, I imagined what could happen.

If Cali were to refuse to accept my request, I would find a place where no one would be in danger except the two of us. Maybe it meant living our lives on the run. And maybe neither of us would be able to see our family again. But it would work. And the two of us could be together.

So when he called and I heard his voice, I knew what I would be doing for the rest of my life. I would be spending it with him. We were going to see every part of the country. Cali would teach me how to camp. And our lives would be each other.

This was what I told Cali before he agreed to drive up to get me. It seemed like a tough existence, but it wouldn't be all bad. I would be taking with me as much cash as I could carry. My family wouldn't miss it.

With it, we could have whatever life we wanted. We could eat anywhere and buy anything. We could get the cutest RV, decorate it like it was our dream home, and eat caviar every night.

I couldn't imagine that would be what Cali would want, though. Knowing him, he would probably want something simple. I looked forward to finding out. I couldn't wait for our new adventure to begin.

With him already on his way to our meeting spot, I waited for the perfect time to leave. I would escape the way I had before. After I did, I would head to the home of my best friend in the world.

It turned out that Dillon hadn't been the one to tell Remy where I was. Remy had figured it out on his own. I could trust my best friend. And when Dillon agreed to do everything he could to help me with my plan, I knew I would love him forever.

I was so happy I would be able to see him one last time before I left. For our escape to be successful,

Cali and I would have to cut ourselves off from our families entirely. When the reality of it sank in, it became harder for me than I thought. As much of an asshole my big brother Remy was, I also loved him. I couldn't have survived my penthouse prison sentence without him.

For a guy covered from neck to wrist in tattoos, he was surprisingly funny. I often wondered who he would have become if he wasn't saddled with the responsibilities of this family and our father. He might have ruled the world. I was going to miss him.

I was also going to miss my parents, but in a different way. I was never able to fully embrace who they were and what they did, but not everyone got to grow up unquestionably loved like I was. I was never going to forget that.

But, however I felt, I knew that what Cali was giving up was so much more. When I asked who would take care of his mother, he said his brothers would. They, like everyone in town, loved his mother. She would always be well taken care of.

I also asked if he thought his mother would understand us leaving. He said she would. He told me that it had something to do with his birth father. I didn't quite understand it and he didn't go into details, but he seemed confident in his decision. He loved me as much as I loved him. I was the luckiest guy in the world.

When it became time for me to leave, I looked around at my room for the last time. I was not going to miss this place. Yes, it had everything a person in confinement could dream of. But being here wasn't living. I was choosing life.

Slowly crossing the penthouse retrieving stacks of cash from their hiding places, I filled the duffel bag that I carried, tossed it across my shoulders, and caused the brief power surge that would give me the time I needed to get on to the elevator and escape without having to turn off the alarm.

It had taken me years to put together my first escape. I had made mistakes, though. The biggest was using my phone. That had been how Remy had tracked me down.

I had kept it off for weeks, and during that time, Remy had thought that he had lost me. He had given up checking my phone's tracker. But as I got more comfortable talking with Dillon, Remy had logged back into the app. It showed him my location down to the inch. That's when he came and got me.

This time, however, I was leaving my phone in my bedroom. I just had to get from downtown Manhattan to New Jersey without it. That was easy enough, right?

After all, hadn't people crossed the city before Google Maps? Sure, it was probably by riding one of the dinosaurs that roamed freely back then. But I could do it too.

And considering I was carrying more cash than most people made in a lifetime, it would be easy. I couldn't imagine how I wouldn't be able to cross downtown New York City with a duffel bag of cash over my shoulders... especially since I was taking the subway.

Having researched the metro routes before abandoning my phone, I memorized all of the trains I had to take to get to New Jersey. I kept a few dollars in my pocket for the ticket. It was going to be a breeze.

At least I thought it was. That was just the first thing I got wrong. Never in my life had I seen a place like a subway station. It was insane. I was going to die.

Was it because I had more money than most people would make it a lifetime strapped across my shoulder? Surprisingly, yes. Who would have guessed? Should I have just taken a taxi?

Luckily, I didn't have much time to think about it. With my ticket in hand, I scurried to the platform and my train quickly pulled up. Rushing in, I found a seat. Hiding in the corner, I witnessed a guy rapping, someone else dancing, I think someone was being mugged, and another person who pooped in the train.

Um, was I making a mistake?

Practically running off of the subway as soon as I arrived at my stop, I went over the map that I had burned into my brain. Deciding that it would be harder to find a taxi than just to walk there, I put on as much attitude as I could and marched forward, barely looking around.

On my way, I thought about how this was going to be my life from now on. Unfamiliar streets, people pooping on subway trains, being lost and kind of terrified—this was my new normal. The thought would have pushed me to step into the nearest store and call my brother to come get me if I didn't then think about the man I was doing all of this to meet.

If this was all I had to do to spend the rest of my life with Cali, I would do it forever. He was worth it. There are times when you can imagine what your life would be if you spend it in someone else's arms. I wanted that life to be my future.

I would want a life with him, even if we began it with nothing. I didn't need fancy restaurants or penthouse suites. All I needed was him. I relaxed as I thought about it.

Knocking on Dillon's door, I was ready.

"Hil!" he said, seeing me in person for the first time in way too long.

We threw our arms around each other. He really was the best friend I could ever have. I wasn't sure what I was going to do without him. Tears filled my eyes thinking about it.

"When you told me you would be taking the subway, I wondered if you would get here in one piece,"

Dillon joked as he ushered me in and chain locked the door.

"What are you talking about? It was nothing."

He looked at me doubtingly.

"You took the train from downtown to New Jersey, and you didn't see anything out of the ordinary?"

I remained poker faced.

"No. Like what?"

"Lying does not look good on you. Does your boyfriend know you lie like this?"

"He knows everything about me. And whatever he doesn't know, he is about to find out," I said with a hint of nervousness.

"Are you sure about this, Hil? You will be giving up a lot if you go through with it."

"He's coming here so you're gonna meet him. You can see for yourself if he's worth giving everything up for," I said confidently.

"Well, I hope he is. And don't forget, if it doesn't work out, you have a home where people love you," he said sadly.

I threw my arms around him again.

"Thank you. But I promise you, he's worth giving everything up for."

Sitting on the couch, we lean against each other. Dillon sniffed.

"I can't believe you're leaving me."

"I can't believe it either. I love you, Dillon. I'm going to miss you so much," I said sniffing as well.

"I would say that I'm just a FaceTime away but…"

I swallowed, trying to hold myself together and then, impulsively, I threw my arms around his neck. This guy had been everything to me. For so long, he was my entire world. I probably wouldn't have survived without him in my life. And now I was leaving him. Was I making a mistake?

Hearing a knock on the door, I let him go. Glancing between the door and Dillon, my heart hurt.

"That's him. That's my man," I said through a tearful smile.

"You're at least going to introduce me, right?" Dillon said, wiping his eyes.

"Of course. I want the two most important people in my life to meet each other," I said, straightening myself up.

"Then go do it," Dillon said, gesturing towards the door. "Let him into our life."

Gathering myself, I stood up, made the short walk to the front door, and threw it open. Terror filled me as I stared through it.

Standing on the other side of it was not Cali. I didn't know who it was. The one thing I did know was that I had made a horrible mistake. This man was not here to help me. This was the man who had wanted me dead.

Chapter 18

Cali

Driving into the city was unlike anything I could imagine. Everything was overwhelming. Without giving it a second thought, I left my entire world behind. I didn't worry about Mama. Thanks to Titus and Claude, she would be in better hands than she would have been with me.

But Mama had made me promise that I would finish getting my college degree. I couldn't do that now. Even if I could somehow do my classes online while we traveled to wherever we ended up, I couldn't afford to attend because I was only there on a football scholarship.

That was another thing, people were starting to talk about me going pro. I wouldn't have been the first from my small town to get that opportunity, of course. Cage had the chance to go pro and he turned it down for Quin. His brother, on the other hand, was playing for the NFL. And after the damage he did this past season, Titus would also have that option; though I think he'll turn it down to be mayor of Snow Tip Falls.

So, that brings it back to me. This year as a freshman, I broke records as a kicker. The college ranks had never seen anything like me. Cage was my high school coach and had helped me get my scholarship. I was pretty sure that if I asked him, he would connect me with his brother, and Nero would help me with anything I needed to enter the draft.

I was giving all of that up, though. And I didn't regret it. The only thing that mattered to me was Hil. I was going to get to be with him. As long as I had him in my arms, nothing else mattered.

Would giving everything up be hard? Definitely. But would having a lifetime with Hil make up for it? You're god damn right it would.

Following the last of the directions appearing on my phone, I was about to arrive. I had been driving for nearly two days straight. The only time I slept was when it became dangerous for everyone else on the road. That was when I parked in a rest stop, tilted my chair back, and took a quick nap.

I didn't need to rest now. I couldn't be more excited for my new life to begin. The first thing I was going to do was scoop him into my arms and find his lips. I wanted to taste him. I wanted to feel his soft curls in my hand and his gentle cheek pressed against my palm.

When our tongues danced, I would know that I'm home. I loved that man so much it hurt. Parking, and sprinting up the stairs to his friend's floor, I felt like I was about to explode.

I slowed when counting the room numbers, I approached a door that was open. It wasn't just cracked, the door was thrown to the side. This was the apartment I was supposed to meet Hil in. Wait, what the fuck was going on?

Staring from the hallway, I saw two people. One person sat bleeding on the couch and the other stood in front of him glaring down. The bigger guy looked like a monster.

From behind, I saw straight through him. Crisp white shirt, slicked back hair—this guy was pretending to be someone he wasn't. And when he turned around and locked eyes with mine, I knew he was about to die by my hands.

"You," he said to me as I rushed in preparing for the tackle.

He had made a mistake by not protecting himself. Grabbing him, I lifted him up and slammed him onto a coffee table as hard as I could. The table shattered beneath him. And before he could gather himself I went to work.

With him pinned down, I tried to break his face with my fist.

"What did you do with Hil?" I said, intentionally not giving him a chance to reply. "Tell me what you did with him," I demanded.

"Stop!" the guy on the couch implored. "Don't hurt him. Stop!"

Nothing was going to stop me from pounding him into oblivion. As I did, something clicked. I recognized him. It was the guy who had stolen Hil from me back in Snow Tip Falls. So, I had a new reason to pummel the life out of him. Nothing was going to stop me now. He was going to be a bloody mess by the time I was done.

That was when something unexpected happened. The guy who was bleeding on the couch, threw himself at me. What was he doing? Was I going to have to fight the both of them?

It didn't matter. Whatever it took. Throwing the smaller guy off of me, I saw something change in the big guy's eyes. There was rage. I had awoken the devil.

While I was off balance, he pulled from under me. Suddenly it was a fair fight. When he grabbed my throat and threw himself on me, I worked my knee between us and punted him off. Rising to his feet, he stumbled back. Climbing to my knees, I looked at him like I was about to devour him.

With nothing but darkness in my eyes, I rushed towards him, only to be halted by the outstretched arms of the smaller guy.

"Cali, stop! This is Hil's brother. Hil wouldn't want you two fighting," he said screaming at me loud enough for it to sink in.

That's right. Hil had said that the person who had taken him had been his brother. That's who this man was. Catching myself, I looked around for Hil.

"Where is he?" I growled.

"Because of you, someone took him," the man growled back.

I didn't like the guy in front of me. I didn't like the way he looked. I didn't like what he said. But, the smaller guy was right. Hil wouldn't want me fighting with him. And that was the last thing I should be doing if something had happened to the man I loved.

Stepping back like a tamed wolf, I stared at Hil's brother, waiting for him to make a move. Although he stared back, he didn't challenge me. As the fire between us burned out, I released my balled-up fists and straightened my back.

"What do you mean he was taken because of me?" I asked as his words sunk in.

"If the asshole wasn't stupid enough to meet some hillbilly and try to run off with him, he would be at home safe right now."

"I don't care who you are, don't you ever talk about Hil like that. You hear me?" I said, ready to shoot across the room and finish what I started.

"Seriously, Cali, calm down. Everyone here wants the same thing. We just want to find him and make sure he's safe," the little one said.

I looked over at him.

"Are you Dillon?"

"Yeah. And this is his brother Remy. And you're the guy that he was going to leave us for. Now that we've established who everyone is, how about we stop waving our dicks around and get to helping the person we all care about?"

As much as I didn't like the way he said it, Dillon was probably right. If something had happened to Hil, I wouldn't know the first place to start. Nashville was the largest city I'd ever been in. It was no New York.

"What do we do?" I said, ready to do whatever I had to.

"I can tell you what you can do," Hil's brother said, glaring at me. "You can get back into your truck and drive back to whatever pumpkin patch you climbed out of," he said imitating my accent.

"Not gonna happen," I told him making sure he knew that they weren't going anywhere without me.

"Oh yeah?" he said, taking a step towards me.

"You heard me," I said readying myself for another fight.

"For God's sake! Can you both just put it back in your pants?" Dillon said, calming things. "Look, Remy, like it or not, this is the guy that Hil loves. He's told me everything about him, and from what I hear, Hil will never do better. He's seriously not going to leave without getting Hil back."

He then turned to me. "And you Mr. *I run in without first asking questions*, this is Hil's brother, Remy. You really don't want to mess with him."

"I—"

"Seriously! You do not know who you're dealing with. So why don't we all just sit down and figure this out. The longer you two bicker, the more likely it is that we don't get him back alive."

That did it. It's sobered me up real quick. We were dealing with whether or not the guy I loved survived the night. This wasn't a game. I couldn't be acting like this.

"You're right. I'm sorry," I said to Dillon. "And you," I said turning to Remy. "I know that you only have Hil's best interest at heart. I shouldn't have come at you ready to throw down. Let's just get him back safe. Tell me what I need to do. I'll do whatever I have to do to help."

"Then go home."

"Anything but that," I said firmly.

"Remy! Let it go. Isn't this the type of person you would want in a fight? Someone who's willing to do whatever it takes to get your brother back?"

The tattooed asshole looked like he hated me. I was oaky with that. When he accepted that I wasn't going anywhere, we retreated to the small round dinner table that was pressed up against one of the apartment's sparsely decorated walls.

"Fine," the asshole said, interlocking his fingers and leaning forward. "I've made a few calls."

"And?" I asked.

As soon as my contact knows anything, he'll call me back."

"And in the meantime?"

"I don't know. Maybe we fight whatever country bumpkin comes in after him next," he said with a smirk large enough to burrow under my skin.

How could Hil and this guy be related? The two were nothing alike. Hil was the sweetest, kindest person I'd ever met. This guy was a hyena off his leash. The difference was mind boggling.

Not responding to his comment, I leaned back not saying a word. Hil's safety was the only thing that was important right now. Maybe when this was all over, we could finish what we started. Until then, I just had to put up with it.

As the silence drew out, I could see Hil's friend becoming uncomfortable. It was unfortunate. I was hoping that the two of us would get along. Hil had gotten along so well with my people. I wanted him to see that I could get along with his.

"You really are everything Hil said you were," Dillon said, staring at me.

"How long did you know about the two of them?" Remy asked him.

"Hil is my best friend. He told me as soon as it happened."

"So all those times I called you asking if you knew where Hil was, what? You were lying to me."

Dillon looked away guiltily.

"Believe me, I didn't want to. But he asked me to."

"And you're always loyal to your friends?"

Gathering his courage, he stood up to Remy.

"That's right. Do you have a problem with that?"

The asshole smirked.

"No. I'm just sitting here wondering how I could become one of them."

I stared at the two very confused about what I was seeing. Remy was staring at him while Dillon's cheeks turned red.

"Are you two fucking flirting?" I asked pissed off.

"No!" Remy said seeming caught off guard.

"No," Dillon replied with a lot less conviction.

It was then that Remy's phone rang. Quickly answering it, he said, "What do you have? Uh-huh. I got it. Thanks," he said, ending the call. "He's still alive and he's being held by one of my family's rivals."

"It's the guy who tried to kill him," I said.

"Yeah, I heard about that. That was probably the guy who took him. The guy holding him is the one who ordered the hit."

"What do we do?" I asked.

"I go there and negotiate," he said soberly.

I corrected him.

"We go there and negotiate."

He looked at me coldly.

"There's a good chance someone's gonna end up dead. If you want to be the cannon fodder, I would love not to die tonight."

I swallowed, allowing the reality of what was going on to sink in.

"Whatever it takes," I told him.

"Damn! My brother really did find a crazy one," Remy said, almost sounding impressed.

I wasn't going to acknowledge the asshole's bullshit. If I was gonna die tonight, I didn't feel like wasting the words.

Turned out, his plan really was to get me killed. Knowing where Hil was being held, the two of us were just gonna walk into the place. And after I told him how good I was with a shot gun, he looked at me and laughed.

"You think that we're going to keep my brother alive by going in cowboy style? Jesus, you really don't know anything, do you? No. I told you, we're going there to negotiate. If you decide to do anything crazy, I'll kill you myself. My brother means a whole lot more to me than he does to you. I will do anything to make sure that he's the one who walks out of there alive."

"Then, we're in agreement. Because that's what I plan on too," I said, staring into the thug's eyes.

With Remy clear about where I stood, he and I left Dillon's apartment for his car. He was driving what he had stuffed his brother into back at Snow Tip Falls. I had never been in such a fancy car before. Considering Remy was acting like he had no intention in allowing me to survive the night, the vehicle was fitting. It was like getting to choose your final meal. It was a bit of luxury before the end.

Speeding our way through the New York streets, I began to realize that Remy was insane. I was then sure of it when after parking outside of a high-rise building, he flipped down the sun visor, opened the vanity mirror, and adjusted his hair.

Was he kidding?

"Making sure you look pretty?" I asked, wondering what the hell he was doing.

He looked at me like he had a rat stuck in his ass.

"When you go into a negotiation, you don't go in looking weak; you look your best."

He glanced at what I was wearing. "Or, whatever it is you have going on there."

"Asshole," I said.

"Redneck," he retorted

At least we knew where we both stood.

Following him as he left the car, I adjusted my flannel shirt and beat up jeans. I didn't have much to work with. But if it meant getting Hil out of this unharmed, I was willing to try my best.

Remy saw me squirming and didn't comment. I didn't like him thinking he had gotten the better of me and had made me feel self-conscious, so I appreciated him not pointing it out. Maybe he wasn't a complete asshole after all.

Entering the building like we owned the place, Remy made a beeline to the person sitting behind the desk.

"Two to see Arnaud Clément. He should be expecting us," Remy said as if we were meeting him to share a beer.

The short, mustached man picked up his phone and made a call. Remy didn't look at him but I couldn't help watch what was going on. This whole thing felt insane. We were going there to rescue the guy I loved, and everyone was treating it like an annoying business transaction. I was in a different world. I truly didn't know what I was dealing with.

"You can take the elevator to the 30th floor," the guy behind the desk said before the elevator dinged.

Following Remy onto it, I waited for the doors to close and then looked at him. He was my height and a big guy, but he was shaped differently than I was. My muscles were rounded like you would be after years of football practice. He was built like he had spent years chiseling his body in a gym.

He was like a pretty boy who had learned how to defend himself. Hell, he could more than just defend himself. If Dillon hadn't separated us, it would have been quite the fight.

"Is there a reason you're staring at me?" he said with his eyes locked forward.

"I'm wondering what it is you plan on doing. Are you just gonna offer me up in exchange for Hil and go? Or are you gonna stick around and watch them torture me to death?"

"People pay good money to watch stuff like that," he said considering. "I guess I'll decide in a moment," he said, turning to me and smiling like the snake he was.

"Fuck you."

"Fuck you too," he retorted before the elevator dinged and the doors opened.

What lay before us was nothing I could have prepared for. We were staring at a living room whose carpet was covered with a blue tarp. In the center of it was a chair. Tied to it with his mouth taped shut was Hil.

There was dried blood on the corner of his eye. Someone had hit him. I stepped forward, ready to pound the shit out of anyone who tried to stop me. As I did, Remy stuck out his arm blocking my path.

"Unless you're hoping to get my brother killed, I suggest you calm the fuck down right now," he said staring at me.

Listening to him, I took a breath. This was all about keeping Hil safe.

Stepping out of the elevator and into the foyer, I spotted the two guys with their guns drawn. They were staring at us. Yep, I had been seconds away from getting myself killed. The asshole had just saved my life.

"Mr. Lyon. So nice of you to join us," an older, menacing guy said.

Although the man couldn't take me in a fight, it was clear that he had been in many of them. With a face full of healed scars and a body rounded from indulgence, it wasn't someone to be messed with.

"Mr. Clement. Your invitation was hard to ignore."

"I see that you got it," he said, looking across the room at the love of my life. "And who's this? Don't you know it's rude to invite the uninvited?" he said giving me the once over.

"Well, there are some things that can't be avoided. You know how that goes."

"I sure I do. So, shall we get down to business? I have something your father wants. And your father has something I want. What do we do about it?"

Remy looked at his little brother strapped to the chair and then turned to the guy who put him there.

"Well, the first thing you can do is untie my brother before I reach in your throat and rip out your tongue," Remy said with a darkness in his eyes that I couldn't have imagined.

The guy stared at him measuring the situation.

I thought we were about to be shot to death until the guy said, "Come now. You can do better than that. Sit, share a drink with me," he said gesturing to the couch casually.

I seriously did not know what was going on. Was that how these people said hello? The crazier thing was that Remy went to the couch while gesturing for me to stay. They were actually going to share a drink together while Hil sat covered in blood and scared out of his mind.

With the two of them sitting on the couch, one of the guy's men came over with a bottle of wine and showed his boss the label. His boss nodded, and as the two watched, the guy opened the bottle and poured two glasses.

"As if it were the most normal thing in the world, Remy took a sip and complemented it.

"Chateau Margaux 2014?"

"2015, actually. You know your wine," the man said impressed.

"I know the things that are important."

"Then I hope you know what's important to me."

"You want what you've always wanted, to control my father's territory," Remy said casually.

"No, I want the territory your father took from me. And I want compensation for the trouble."

Remy swirled the wine around in his glass as if it were the only thing in the room.

"I'm assuming you've heard about my father's condition?"

"I might have heard something about it," the older man said with a smile.

"You do know that I am more than capable of defending everything my father has built?"

"That I don't doubt. What I doubt is your willingness to sacrifice your brother to do it. As you see, I also have a knack for knowing what's important."

Remy conceded with a shrug.

"Then how about this. I acknowledge our defeat. I will let you take over all of my father's off-the-book activities. That includes his protection routes, backroom bars, and his numbers businesses."

"In exchange for what?" he asked, having Remy's full attention.

"In exchange for letting my brother go and guaranteeing us the protection that such a gesture would earn. I want no one coming after me, my brother, my mother, or any of our remaining businesses. And I want you to treat us like a member of the family."

"A distant member?" the older man clarified.

"A member that you know could slice your throat if ever you backed out on the deal," Remy said calmly.

The man thought about it for a second.

"Then, it's a deal."

"Excellent. You do understand that none of this will kick in until my father, God rest his soul, is no longer with us."

"Of course. I would never want to insult family," he said with a smile.

"Excellent," he said before swigging the wine and getting up from the couch.

"There's only one more thing to deal with."

"What's that?" Remy said as he was about to approach Hil to untie him.

"My compensation for the trouble," he said, pulling out his gun.

Remy stared at him like a wolf about to pounce.

"Don't do anything stupid. You got what you want. Walk away."

"Come on, Remy. You know that's not the way this works. Your father insulted me. I can't let him die thinking he got the better of me. I demand my pound of flesh."

"Don't do this!" Remy demanded.

"I demand my pound of flesh!" he screamed like a madman.

"Take me!" I yelled, drawing his attention.

He relaxed. "What?"

My heart was beating a thousand miles an hour.

"You heard me. If you need to take flesh, take mine."

The man looked at Remy confused.

"I'm sorry, who is this?"

"He's the man that loves my brother," Remy told him, catching me off guard.

Looking at Remy for a moment, I turned back to the older guy.

"That's right. I love his brother and I'm not gonna let you do anything to him," I said ready to die.

He looked at me trying to puzzle everything together.

"So, this is someone who means something to your family?"

Remy wasn't quick to answer, but soon he nodded his head. "Yeah. He means a lot."

"Good enough," he said before lifting his gun and shooting me.

Chapter 19

Hil

The explosion that followed the gunshot ripped through me like I was made of paper. The man I loved, and would do anything for, moved in slow motion. Every painful twitch that rippled through his body tore through mine.

Swept off his feet, he hits the ground in anguish. Cali had been shot. I had gotten him killed.

"This is why we lay the tarp," the murderer said as he casually turned to a henchman. "Now he is going to get blood all over my carpet."

Fire burned through me hearing his heartless words. I wanted him dead. I wanted everyone dead. He couldn't be allowed to get away with doing this to someone as good and kind as Cali. There had to be consequences. And when I looked at Remy, I knew he thought the same thing.

Stunned, my brother stared at Cali. I don't know how they met or ended up here together, but Remy reacted like Cali meant something to him. When he found my eyes, I realized that it was because Cali meant something to me, and he felt it.

Staring at me, it was like he could read my mind. I never approved of my brother's acts of violence, even when they were in my defense. But here and now, they were justified. He could tell what I wanted him to do, whatever the consequences.

Hardening his jaw and reaching behind his back, I was about to get what I desired when I heard the only voice that could bring me back.

"I'm okay," Cali said, drawing my attention.

I didn't see where the bullet had hit him, but as he attempted to get off the floor, it became clear. My father's rival had shot him in the leg. Cali was a football player whose specialty was kicking the ball. The bullet might have ruined his life, but it wouldn't take it.

"I think I'm fine," he said, bringing tears of relief.

I could breathe again. My world wasn't coming to an end. All I wanted now was to get out of here and take care of the person I wanted to spend the rest of my life with. He had taken a bullet for me. I could never have imagined anyone like him. The pain I felt from my love for him was overwhelming. All I wanted was to climb inside of him and warm myself with his heart.

For that to happen, it meant that Remy couldn't get us all killed. I quickly whipped my gaze to him. He still had his hand behind his back. I could practically feel his finger on the trigger.

I was begging him not to do it but he was no longer looking at me. He was locked on his target. I didn't know what he was about to do.

"Of course you're alright. I said a pound of flesh, not the whole hog," Armand said casually.

Letting his handgun drop to his side, he looked at Remy. There was no missing what was in my brother's eyes. Armand didn't overreact.

"So, what do you say? Have we made a deal or shall we continue our negotiation?" he said before his two henchmen lifted their guns and pointed it at Remy.

Knowing that I had a chance at spending a long life with the man I loved, I groaned, begging for Remy's attention. When he looked at me, I did everything I could to show him how I felt. I wanted to walk out of here. I wanted it to be with Cali and Remy. And I wanted the life that my brother had negotiated. I wanted it more than anything.

As I pleaded with him with my eyes, I saw the guy I grew up with reveal the tenderness he always tried to hide. The hand that was behind his back, returned to his side.

"We have a deal. But the minute you don't live up to your side of the bargain, know that you won't see me coming."

"I would expect nothing less," Armand said with all of the charm in the world. "And know that if I do decide to change the parameters of our arrangement, you would be the first person to know," he said pointing his gun at Remy and pretending to shoot.

My brother didn't appreciate that but luckily, he decided to let it go.

"Release my brother," he demanded.

Armand signaled for his two henchmen to holster their pistols and release me from the chair. As soon as I was free, I ran to Cali, who had been struggling to get to his feet.

"For Christ's sake, will you stop dripping blood on my carpet!" the bastard said before leaving us and disappearing into one of the side rooms.

Throwing my arms around Cali as he balanced erect on one foot, I never wanted to let him go.

"I love you. I'm sorry," I kept repeating. "I can't believe this happened to you because of me."

"I'm willing to go through this and more to be with you. I have no life without you. When I found you, I found the other half of my heart. I will never let you go again," he said until I stopped him with a kiss.

Fireworks couldn't outshine the majesty of our kiss. I lost myself in the moment. My thoughts swirled as if it were warm caramel wrapped around his chocolate. I could have stood there holding him forever if I hadn't heard,

"Now you're just rubbing it in," Remy said, drawing me back to earth. "How about we get out of here so you can keep all of that behind closed doors?"

Still holding Cali, I looked back at my brother. He had that devilish smirk on his face. I couldn't tell if he was trying to be an asshole or sweet. But he was right, we did have to get out of here. So, helping Cali up, I stepped under his arm to take his weight.

When Cali struggled, Remy rolled his eyes and said, "Fine." And then he displaced me and wrapped my boyfriend's arms around his shoulder. It was Remy who helped Cali out. I could barely express what I felt seeing it.

This was my family, and I was so grateful for it. Remy never liked anyone. So for him to treat my guy like this was beyond my wildest dreams.

Opening the elevator, and later the door to the building, I led two of my three favorite guys out.

"Are we going to Dillon's place? He got hit pretty good fighting the guy who took me. Is he all right?"

"He's fine," Remy replied quickly. "He's quite the scrapper. Who knew he had that in him?"

"I did. You just don't know because you haven't been paying attention."

"Maybe I need to rectify that."

I turned to my brother, scanning his face for what he meant by that. The last thing I wanted was for my womanizing brother to hurt my gay best friend. I knew Dillon had a crush on him. I guess I could see why. My brother was pretty great. But he was also extremely straight.

But Dillon was a lot of things, a good judge of character wasn't one of them. He made the worst choices when it came to men. What was his obsession with straight guys?

"Don't play with his heart," I said sternly.

"Hil, I thought you knew me better than that."

"I do know you. That's why I said it," I told him, not liking the look on his face.

Putting that aside, we helped Cali into Remy's car. Applying pressure to his wound, we drove back to my family's penthouse. We had a medic on staff to take care of stuff this because, of course we did. And he was waiting for us when Remy and I helped Cali out of our elevator and into my room.

"So, this is where you grew up?" Cali asked, scanning the embarrassing posters on my walls.

"If I knew you were coming, I might have moved a few things around," I said hiding my humiliation.

"No, it's good that I've seen the half-naked men plastering your walls. Now I never have to question if you're gay," he said teasing me. "If you had those posters with the lilies, I might have worried."

I chuckled.

Having had his wound dressed and been put on painkillers, I knew he was mine for the night. I had to take off his pants for the doctor. So now there was a hot, half-naked man lying in my bed. Considering how many times I looked at my walls fantasizing about exactly this as a kid, I could barely tell if I was dreaming.

When I cuddled up next to him and gently rolled my fingertips over his rippling muscles, I knew that I wasn't. When my hand found his hardening cock, I realized how much better reality was than a dream. As I gently squeezed it, I looked up into his eyes. Squeezing it harder and gently stroking him, he closed his eyes and lifted his chin.

"If you're in too much pain…" I began before he cut me off.

"Don't you dare stop!"

Liking what I heard, I shifted, getting more comfortable.

"I guess that means I'll have to figure out how to thank you for saving my life."

His thick cock flinched hearing my words.

"I trust you'll find a way," he told me before I pulled back the sheet covering him and did what I had wanted to do since the day I left him.

Gently climbing between his legs, I rested my cheek on his underwear-covered cock. I loved the feeling of it pressed against me. Rolling my face over it, I touched it with the tip of my nose. Tracing its long lines, I next pulled at his underwear with my teeth.

I needed him inside of me. So, gripping my fingers underneath his waistband, I pulled off his underwear. And with nothing between us but my lust and his throbbing manhood, I wrapped my small hand around his thickness and plunged his tip into my mouth. It only took his tip to fill me. My man was so huge.

Wrapping my second hand around his pole, I slowly stroked him. As I did, I traced the rim of his cap with the tip of my tongue. Feeling him flinch with pleasure made my body tingle. So when I tugged him harder, rotating my hands as I did, his moans almost made me explode.

This wasn't how my first encounter with a guy in my bedroom was going to end, though. Cali was my dream guy. His cock was more magnificent than any guy deserved. I needed him inside of me. His size had been a revelation. Feeling him push into me drove me crazy. So retrieving the lube I kept under my bed, I slathered him up and sat with him perched on the entrance of my hole.

This was when I paused and looked down into the eyes of the man I loved. I couldn't understand how I had gotten so lucky. Leaning down to kiss him, I quickly returned to his gaze. My life was perfect when I was with him. Savoring the moment for just a second longer, I then shifted back allowing his oversized monster to enter me.

Together, we moved as if made for each other. Pushing him deep inside of me, I dug my fingers into his chest. Sitting up to ride him, my head fell back.

The feeling of him was everything. I loved him so much. I could never stop loving him. And as he gripped my sides readying to fill me up, I orgasmed covering him with everything I had.

Out of strength and out of breath, I collapsed onto him with him still deep inside of me. Cali was all man, there was no doubt about it.

As my thoughts swayed as if adrift on an ocean, I imagined our life together. I knew I was going to be happy. We both were. And as we grew up and grew old, there was no doubt in my mind that the two of us would live happily ever after.

Epilogue

Cali

With Hil sleeping in my arms like he was always meant to, I considered where we would go from here. With the deal Remy made, Hil and I no longer needed to go on the run. We could be together. Our lives could be whatever we wanted it to be.

Waking up the next morning, I was grateful for the painkillers. Unfortunately, it hadn't a clean shot. The bullet had nicked my bone as it tore through my thigh.

I was going to need a lot of rehab if I was going to play football again. Luckily, football season was still months off. I would have the end of the semester and all summer to recover.

Staying in bed for the next few days, I was sure to catch everyone up back home on what had happened. Although I still couldn't drive, I assured them I was coming back. Meanwhile, my professors forwarded me my schoolwork and my brothers continued to hold down the fort at home.

The first day I was able to get out of bed, Hil introduced me to the other important man in his life. It was hard to say whether or not his father liked me. He seemed to just tolerate me until Remy told him what I had done. After that, the dying man was certainly grateful even though he made clear that no one would be good enough for his son.

Watching the two of them, I wondered what having a father would be like. Hil's dad was definitely full of flaws. But it was clear that he loved Hil. As rough as his old man was, he also didn't have an issue with his son being gay.

Would my father react the same way if he found out? I was thinking I would never know.

"I need to tell you guys something," Claude said the next time the three were on FaceTime.

"What's up?" Titus asked from our dorm room.

"I just got my mother to talk. My whole life she has avoided the subject, but this time when I brought him up, she spoke."

I froze, suddenly awash in panic. Was Claude saying what I thought he was? Did he find out who our father was?

"What did she say?" I asked hesitantly.

"She gave me a name," he said stunned.

"What is it?" I asked, starting to tremble in fear.

"I wrote it down. I want to get it right," he said looking at a piece of paper.

When he said the name, the blood rushed from my face. I recognized it.

"Does that mean anything to either of you?" Claude asked, staring back at us through his camera's phone.

Titus thought for a moment and then said that it didn't. They both then looked at me.

"No. It doesn't mean anything to me either," I lied, hoping that neither would realize it.

"Well, I typed it into the Internet. Nothing came up."

I didn't say it, but I knew there was a reason why it hadn't.

"Listen, I have to go. Hil needs me for something. I should be heading home in a few days, though. We can talk about it then," I told them, trying to get off of the call as quickly as I could.

Alone in Hil's room, I dropped the phone and pressed my palms against my face. Claude had to have heard it wrong. Or maybe it was my memory that was off. Either way, something wasn't right. That person couldn't be my father. I refused to believe it. I refused to even think about it. So instead, I turned my attention to everything else I had going on.

She had set a date, and with the money Hil gave me, everything was good to go. With Dr. Tom reassuring us that she would eventually make a full recovery, we both felt that Mama was in good hands.

But that left me with only one thing to think about. There was no way that that man was our father. I was going to wait and see what else Claude got before saying more. But if he was the man I was thinking he was, God help me. God help us all.

Thinking about rereading this book? Consider reading it as a male/female story in, the sexy curvy girl romance, 'My Grumpy Boss', a steamy wolf shifter romance in 'The Curvy Wolf's Alpha', or a wholesome romance in 'I Don't Date My Grumpy Boss'.

*****

Sneak Peek:
Enjoy this Sneak Peek of 'Furious Chase':

Furious Chase
(MMF Bisexual Romance)
By
Alex McAnders

Copyright 2021 McAnders Publishing
All Rights Reserved

A secret royal, his bad boy best friend, and the curvy woman they both want, fall into an epic MMF bisexual romance. Sharing a room, and a fake relationship lead to, a first time gay relationship, sizzling encounters, and longtime best friends giving in to their heart-aching passion.

KAT

Katherine couldn't have worse taste in men. After thinking she had found the love of her life, she finds herself stranded on an island in the South Pacific without money or a way of getting home. If she hadn't met Angel, a tall, sizzling hot stranger who offers to rescue her, she might have been there forever. And the only thing he asks in return is for her to pretend to be his fiancé first.

Why would he need someone to do something like that? She didn't know. And when they end up sharing a room together at a nudist resort, and the sparks between them turn into a blazing inferno, what could possibly go wrong?

ANGEL

Angel lives in a world where nothing is ever what it seems… and he loves it. His life would be perfect if not for the occasional complication… the biggest of which is

Chase, the one person he can't escape and who forces him to confront his dark secrets.

So when Angel meets Kat and sees a way to escape Chase, he takes it. But could he have a perfect life without Chase? Or, is his childhood best friend the only one who can rescue him from another of his complications, an unbearably lonely heart?

CHASE
Chase found his purpose early in life. It was to clean up his best friend's messes. He couldn't stop himself. He was hopelessly in love with him. But, how did his old friend feel about him?

Everything Angel did told Chase that he wasn't interested. So, why was Chase still following him around the world protecting Angel from himself? And, when Angel introduces him to his beautiful, new fiancé, what does it mean for the two of them?

Will Kat bring Chase and Angel together, or tear them apart? And, if Angel creates a mess like he always does, will Chase clean it up, or make an unexpected decision that leads to the three of them finding the love they all desperately desire?

'Furious Chase' is a steamy bisexual romance with twists, turns and heat. Loaded with crackling MM, MFM, and MMF scenes that will make your toes curl, it will make you laugh as much as cry before leaving you satisfied with its tear-jerking HEA ending.

Author Promise: Swoon-worthy guys; twisting story; crackling sexual tension

*****

Furious Chase

Seeing this, Kat knew she had to do more. With a hand on either of their thighs, she pushed their knees together. Leaning onto them, she slid out of her chair and between their legs. Easing forward, she sat on their knees.

With her legs spread, their meaty thighs pressed against her flesh between her legs. She hadn't realized it until now, but she was aroused. She wanted to rock her hips back and forth to enjoy it. But this wasn't a night for her pleasure. It was a night for theirs.

Balancing on their knees, Kat moved her hand onto Chase's muscular chest. She couldn't help but explore it as her fingers crawled up. Caressing his neck, she took a light hold of his chin. He had a bit of scruff. She liked that. And leaning towards him, she pulled his face to hers.

With the heat pulsating between them, they kissed. Falling into it, Chase quickly lifted his hand and held her back. He parted his lips and found her tongue. The sensation overtook Kat swirling her mind like melted caramel.

It took everything for Kat to break away. She did, though. And when the pleasure crested and subsided, she opened her eyes and turned to Angel.

"Now you," she said barely above a whisper.

Angel did not hesitate. Leaning forward, he kissed her like his life depended on it. His passion was intense. A chill descended Kat's spine feeling his strong lips on hers. She had remembered this feeling. It was like watching a rainstorm from under her covers. It was hard to let go of, but as she had with Chase, Kat pulled away.

Catching her breath, Kat placed a hand on both of their chests. This was it. This was all she knew how to do. If this didn't work, the two might never be together.

With that thought in mind, she looked up, peered into each of their eyes, and said, "Now, you two."
Read more now

Sneak Peek:
Enjoy this Sneak Peek of 'Until Your Toes Curl':

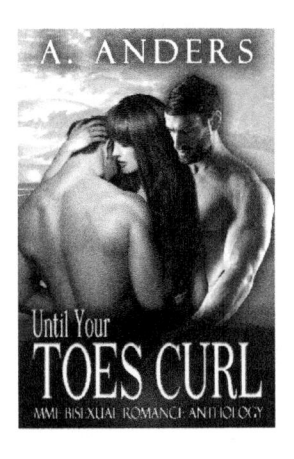

Until Your Toes Curl
(MMF Bisexual Romance)
By
A. Anders

Copyright McAnders Publishing
All Rights Reserved

8 steamy must-have MMF romances about bad boys, billionaires and boyfriends who know how to treat their curvy girls. Closeted guys will have their first loves. Wiser couples will have their second chance at love. Friends will become lovers. And, enemies will become lovers in romances filled with lust, love, endless twists and turns and HEA endings.

Her Best Bad Decision
A cocky baseball player falls for, the off-limits billionaire who owns his team, and the sassy curvy girl who moves in with him uninvited. Laughter follows in this feel-good romance that will have you tearfully cheering for the sexy threesome by the end.

Island Candy (Complete Series)
A billionaire bad boy and a brilliant artist meet their match when they fall for the same untamable girl. Friends become lovers having mind-blowing sex. But it's the emotional connection between the three which leads to a closeted guy's first love. Humor and tears makes this story a tasty treat. (Includes the all new story 'Island Candy: Baby News')

The Muse (Complete Series)
A billionaire businessman and a brilliant artist meet a wild, curvy girl and get their lives turned upside down. A sassy heroine is seduced by a billionaire, while an angsty artist tackles his past. Expect humor, mind-blowing sex, and emotional-fulfillment in this perfect escapist romance.

In The Moonlight (Complete Series)
A genius billionaire, a sexy rocket engineer, and an introverted curvy girl, go on a wild ride towards love.

Dating the boss leads to humor, out of this world sex, and a few tears in this heartwarming romance.

'Until Your Toes Curl' contains very steamy, ultra high heat bisexual menage romance series with explicit MF, MM, MFM and MMF scenes. With lots of humor and twists and turns, each series has a not-to-be-missed HEA ending!

*****

Until Your Toes Curl

Read more now

*****

Follow me on TikTok @AlexAndersBooks where I create funny, fun book related videos:

Printed in Great Britain
by Amazon